TALES FROM BIG SPIRIT

The Rebel
Gabriel Dumont

BY DAVID ALEXANDER ROBERTSON
ILLUSTRATED BY ANDREW LODWICK

HIGHWATER
PRESS

Canada Council   Conseil des arts
for the Arts   du Canada

We acknowledge the support of the Canada Council for the Arts, which last year invested $153 million to bring the arts to Canadians throughout the country.

Nous remercions le Conseil des arts du Canada de son soutien. L'an dernier, le Conseil a investi 153 millions de dollars pour mettre de l'art dans la vie des Canadiennes et des Canadiens de tout le pays.

HighWater Press gratefully acknowledges the financial support of the Province of Manitoba through the Department of Sport, Culture & Heritage and the Manitoba Book Publishing Tax Credit, and the Government of Canada through the Canada Book Fund (CBF), for our publishing activities.

HighWater Press is an imprint of Portage & Main Press.
Printed and bound in Canada by Friesens
Design by Relish New Brand Experience
Map art, inside cover, by Scott Henderson
Literacy consultant: Katya Adamov

Library and Archives Canada Cataloguing in Publication

Robertson, David, 1977-, author
        The Rebel : Gabriel Dumont / David Robertson ; illustrated by Andrew Lodwick.

Issued in print and electronic formats.
ISBN 978-1-55379-476-9 (pbk.).—ISBN 978-1-55379-485-1(pdf).—
ISBN 978-1-55379-486-8 (epub)

        1. Dumont, Gabriel, 1837-1906--Comic books, strips, etc.
2. Dumont, Gabriel, 1837-1906--Juvenile literature. 3. Métis--
Canada, Western--Biography--Comic books, strips, etc. 4. Métis--
Canada, Western--Biography--Juvenile literature. 5. Riel Rebellion,
1885--Comic books, strips, etc. 6. Riel Rebellion, 1885--Juvenile
literature. 7. Graphic novels. I. Lodwick, Andrew, 1980-, illustrator
II. Title.

FC3217.1.D84R62 2013   j971.05'4092   C2013-904842-1
                                                C2013-904843-X

21 20 19 18   3 4 5 6

www.highwaterpress.com
Winnipeg, Manitoba
Treaty 1 Territory and homeland of the Métis Nation

FSC
www.fsc.org
MIX
Paper from responsible sources
FSC® C016245

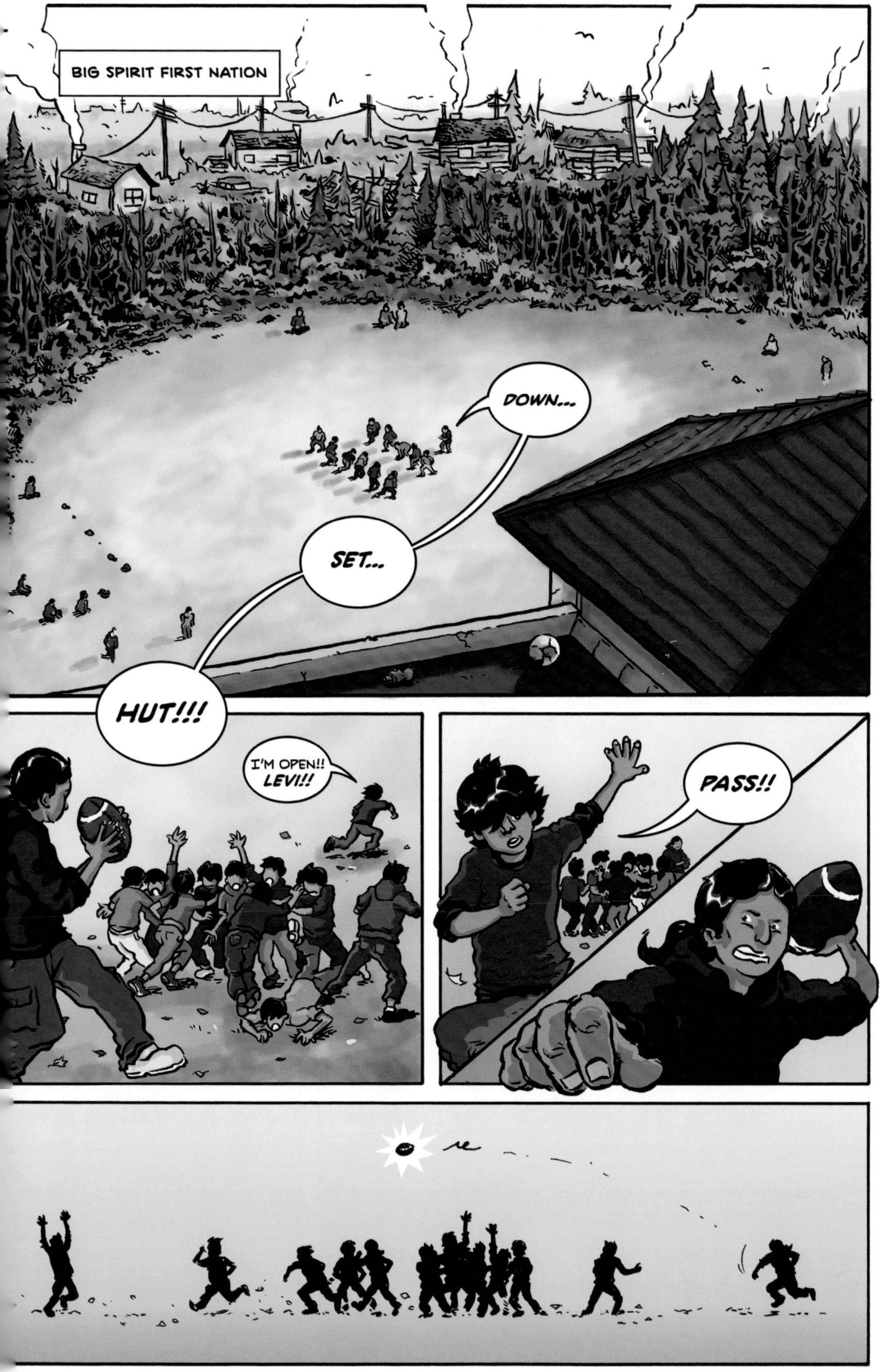
BIG SPIRIT FIRST NATION
DOWN...
SET...
HUT!!!
I'M OPEN!!
LEVI!!
PASS!!

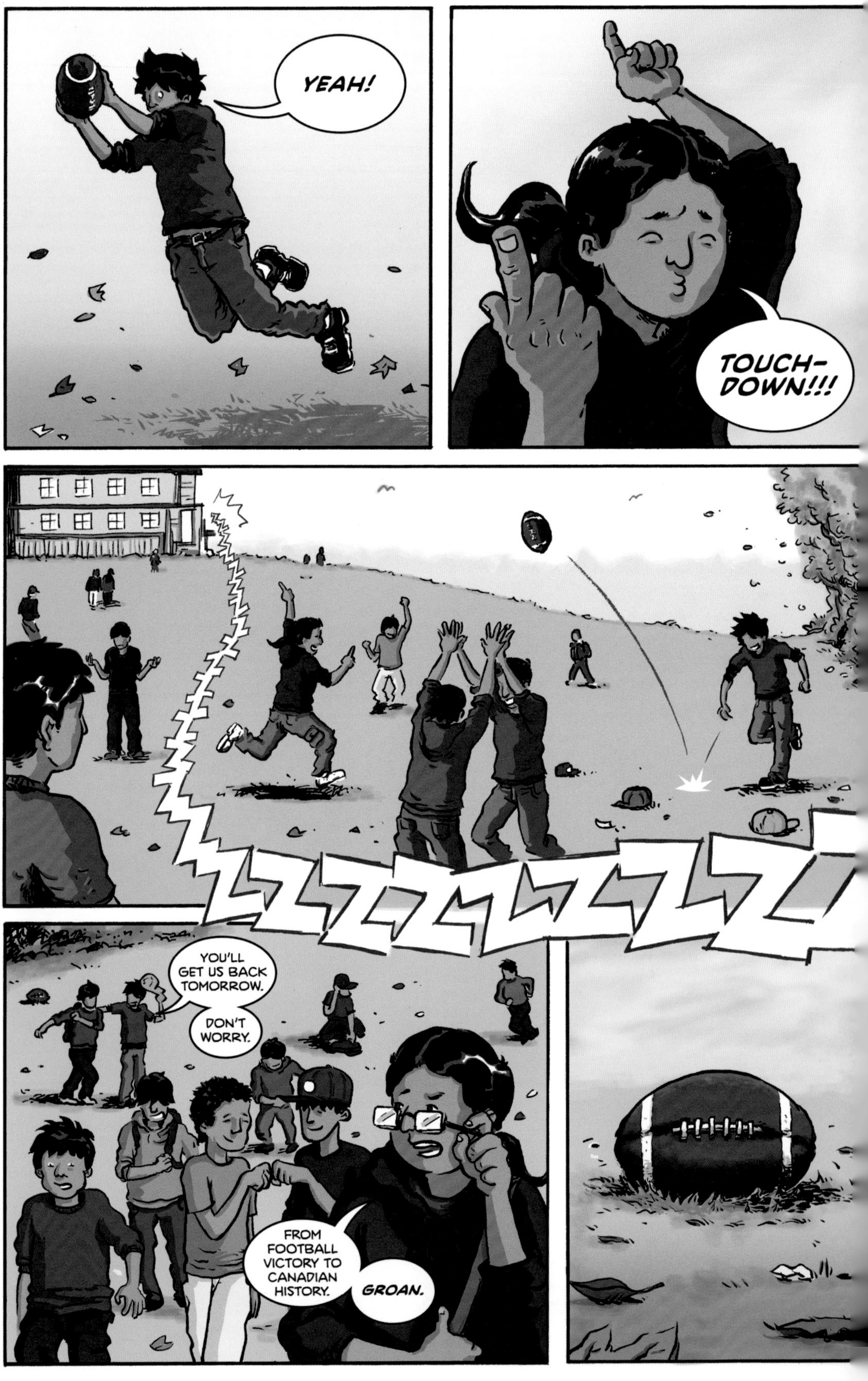
YEAH!
TOUCH-
DOWN!!!
ZZZZZZZZZ
YOU'LL GET US BACK TOMORROW.
DON'T WORRY.
FROM FOOTBALL VICTORY TO CANADIAN HISTORY.
GROAN.

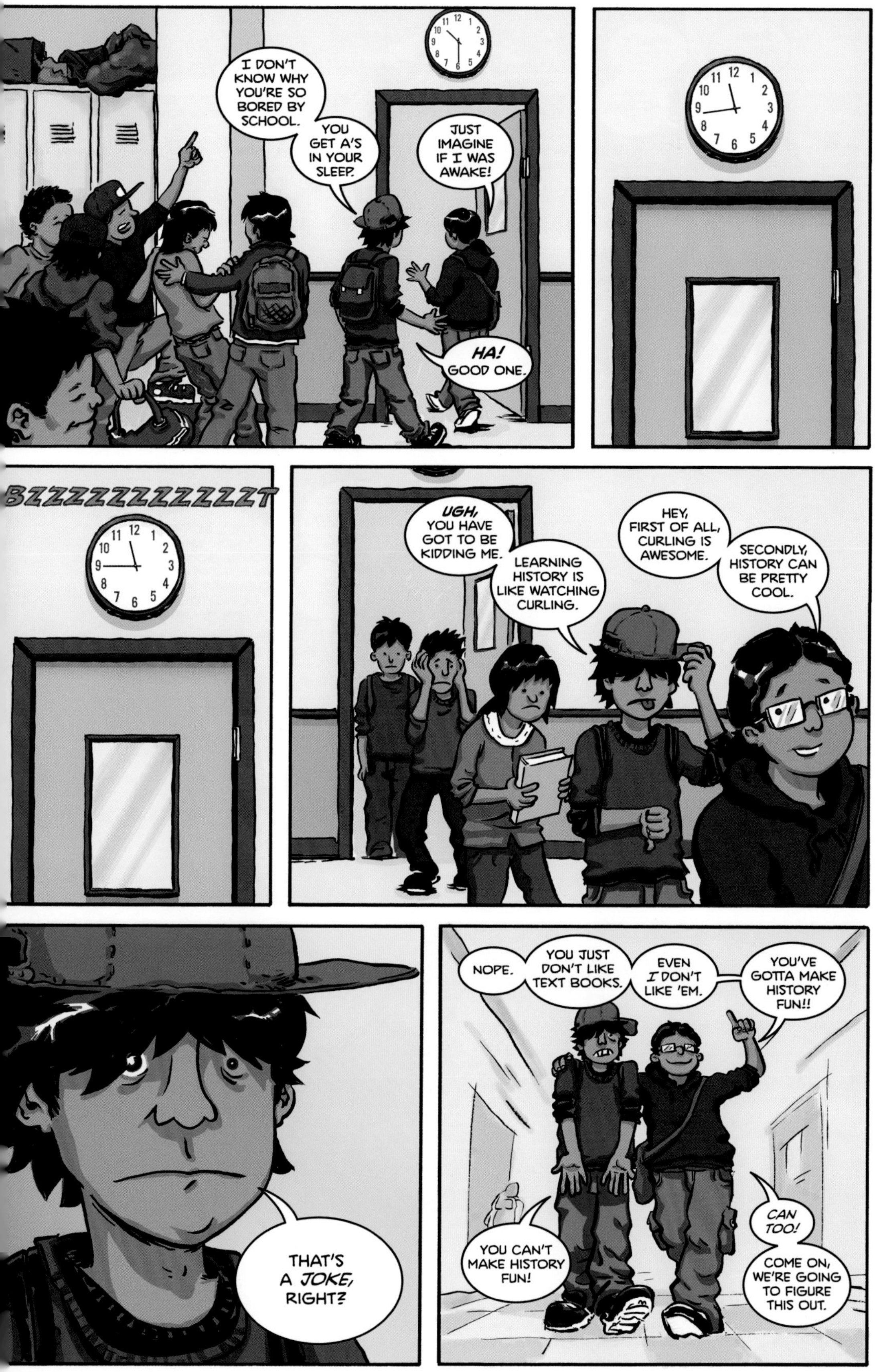
I DON'T KNOW WHY YOU'RE SO BORED BY SCHOOL.
YOU GET A'S IN YOUR SLEEP.
JUST IMAGINE IF I WAS AWAKE!
HA! GOOD ONE.
BZZZZZZZZZZZZT
UGH, YOU HAVE GOT TO BE KIDDING ME.
LEARNING HISTORY IS LIKE WATCHING CURLING.
HEY, FIRST OF ALL, CURLING IS AWESOME.
SECONDLY, HISTORY CAN BE PRETTY COOL.
THAT'S A JOKE, RIGHT?
NOPE.
YOU JUST DON'T LIKE TEXT BOOKS.
EVEN I DON'T LIKE 'EM.
YOU'VE GOTTA MAKE HISTORY FUN!!
YOU CAN'T MAKE HISTORY FUN!
CAN TOO!
COME ON, WE'RE GOING TO FIGURE THIS OUT.

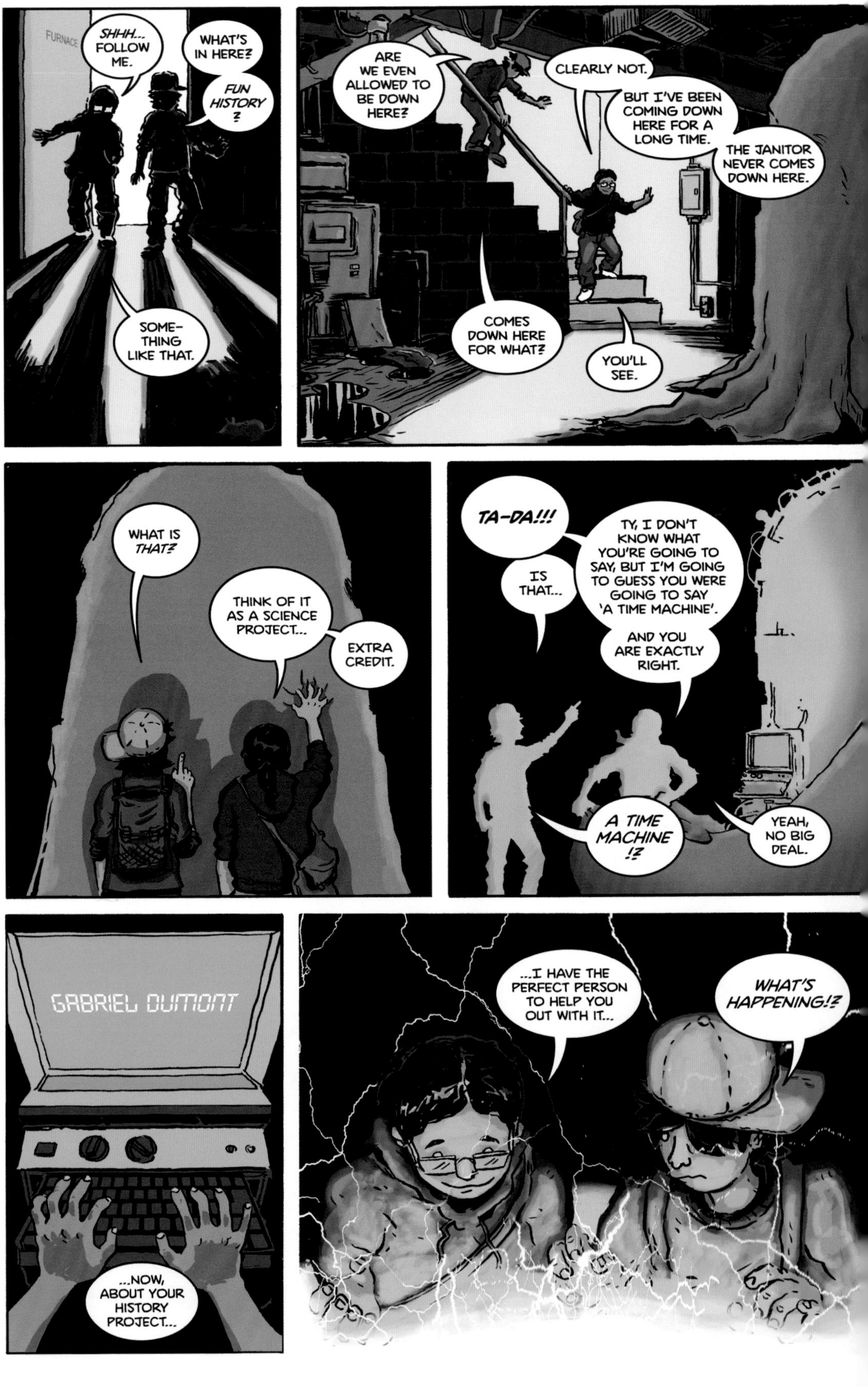
FURNACE
SHHH... FOLLOW ME.
WHAT'S IN HERE?
FUN HISTORY?
SOME-THING LIKE THAT.
ARE WE EVEN ALLOWED TO BE DOWN HERE?
CLEARLY NOT.
BUT I'VE BEEN COMING DOWN HERE FOR A LONG TIME.
THE JANITOR NEVER COMES DOWN HERE.
COMES DOWN HERE FOR WHAT?
YOU'LL SEE.
WHAT IS THAT?
THINK OF IT AS A SCIENCE PROJECT...
EXTRA CREDIT.
TA-DA!!!
IS THAT...
TY, I DON'T KNOW WHAT YOU'RE GOING TO SAY, BUT I'M GOING TO GUESS YOU WERE GOING TO SAY 'A TIME MACHINE'.
AND YOU ARE EXACTLY RIGHT.
A TIME MACHINE!?
YEAH, NO BIG DEAL.
GABRIEL DUMONT
...NOW, ABOUT YOUR HISTORY PROJECT...
...I HAVE THE PERFECT PERSON TO HELP YOU OUT WITH IT...
WHAT'S HAPPENING!?

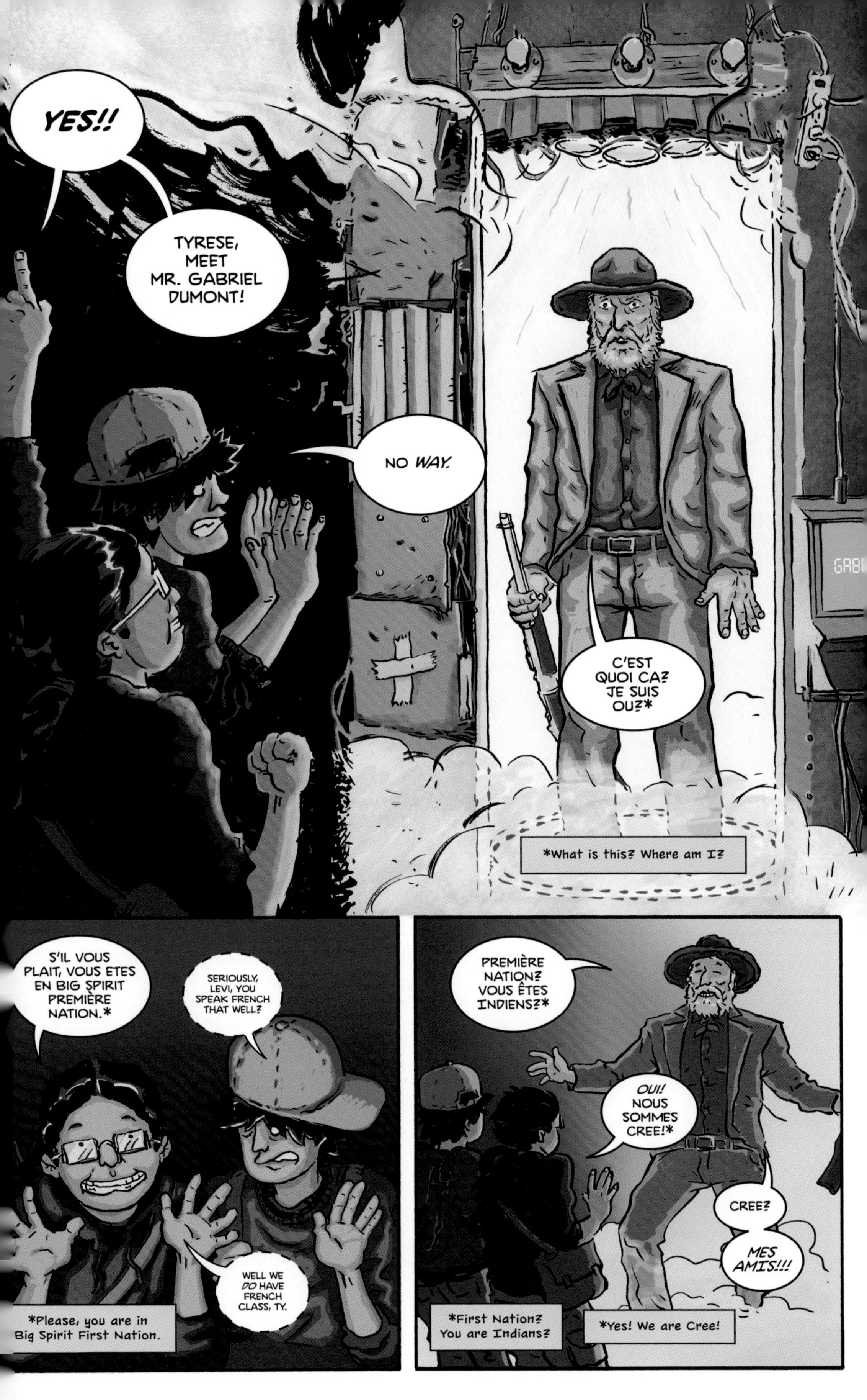
YES!!
TYRESE, MEET MR. GABRIEL DUMONT!
NO WAY.
C'EST QUOI CA? JE SUIS OU?*
*What is this? Where am I?
S'IL VOUS PLAIT, VOUS ETES EN BIG SPIRIT PREMIÈRE NATION.*
SERIOUSLY, LEVI, YOU SPEAK FRENCH THAT WELL?
WELL WE DO HAVE FRENCH CLASS, TY.
*Please, you are in Big Spirit First Nation.
PREMIÈRE NATION? VOUS ÊTES INDIENS?*
OUI! NOUS SOMMES CREE!*
CREE?
MES AMIS!!!
*First Nation? You are Indians?
*Yes! We are Cree!

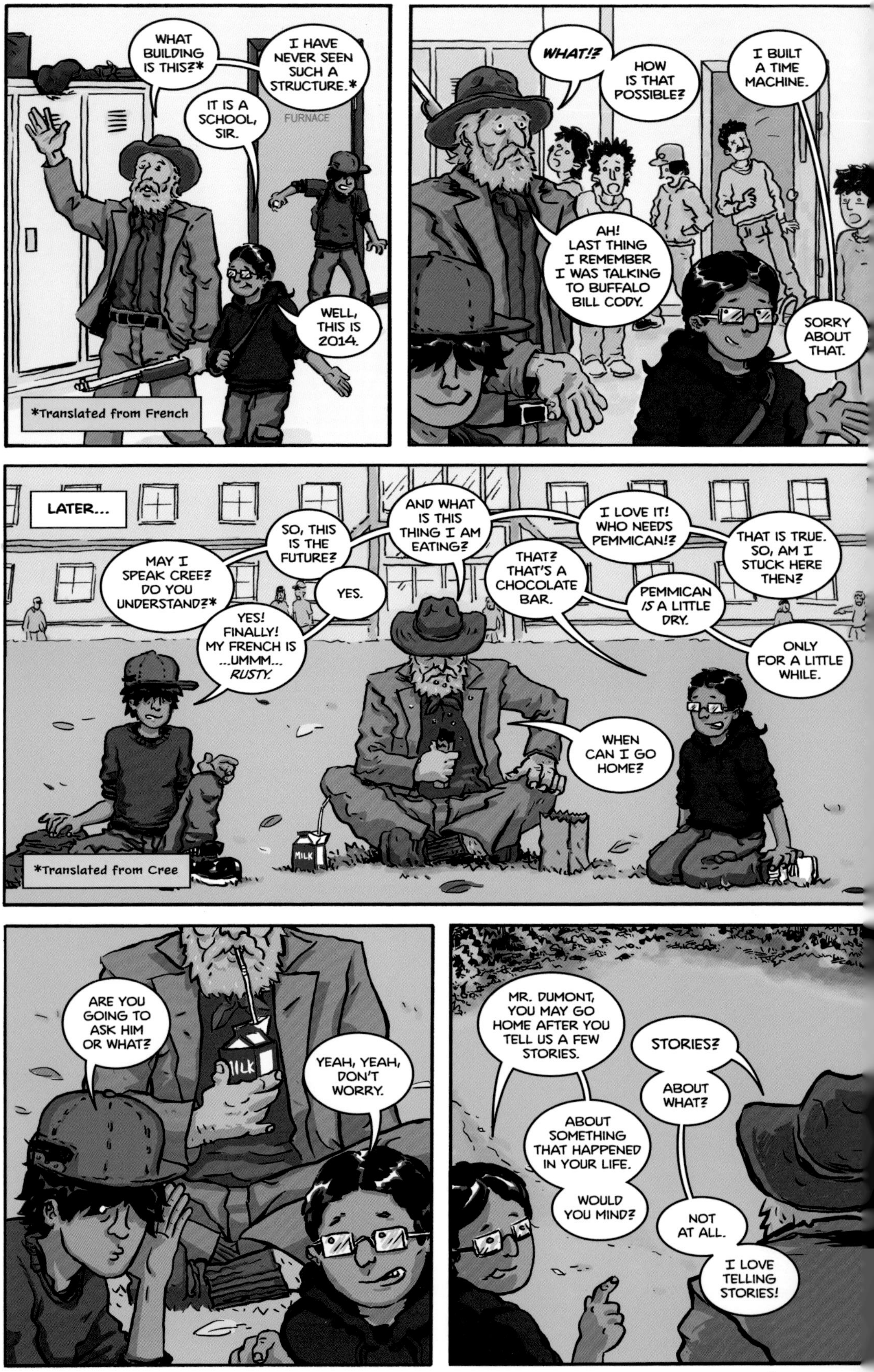
WHAT BUILDING IS THIS?*
I HAVE NEVER SEEN SUCH A STRUCTURE.*
IT IS A SCHOOL, SIR.
FURNACE
WELL, THIS IS 2014.
*Translated from French
WHAT!?
HOW IS THAT POSSIBLE?
I BUILT A TIME MACHINE.
AH! LAST THING I REMEMBER I WAS TALKING TO BUFFALO BILL CODY.
SORRY ABOUT THAT.
LATER...
MAY I SPEAK CREE? DO YOU UNDERSTAND?*
YES! FINALLY! MY FRENCH IS ...UMMM... *RUSTY.*
SO, THIS IS THE FUTURE?
YES.
AND WHAT IS THIS THING I AM EATING?
THAT? THAT'S A CHOCOLATE BAR.
I LOVE IT! WHO NEEDS PEMMICAN!?
PEMMICAN *IS* A LITTLE DRY.
THAT IS TRUE. SO, AM I STUCK HERE THEN?
ONLY FOR A LITTLE WHILE.
WHEN CAN I GO HOME?
MILK
*Translated from Cree
ARE YOU GOING TO ASK HIM OR WHAT?
YEAH, YEAH, DON'T WORRY.
MILK
MR. DUMONT, YOU MAY GO HOME AFTER YOU TELL US A FEW STORIES.
STORIES?
ABOUT WHAT?
ABOUT SOMETHING THAT HAPPENED IN YOUR LIFE.
WOULD YOU MIND?
NOT AT ALL.
I LOVE TELLING STORIES!

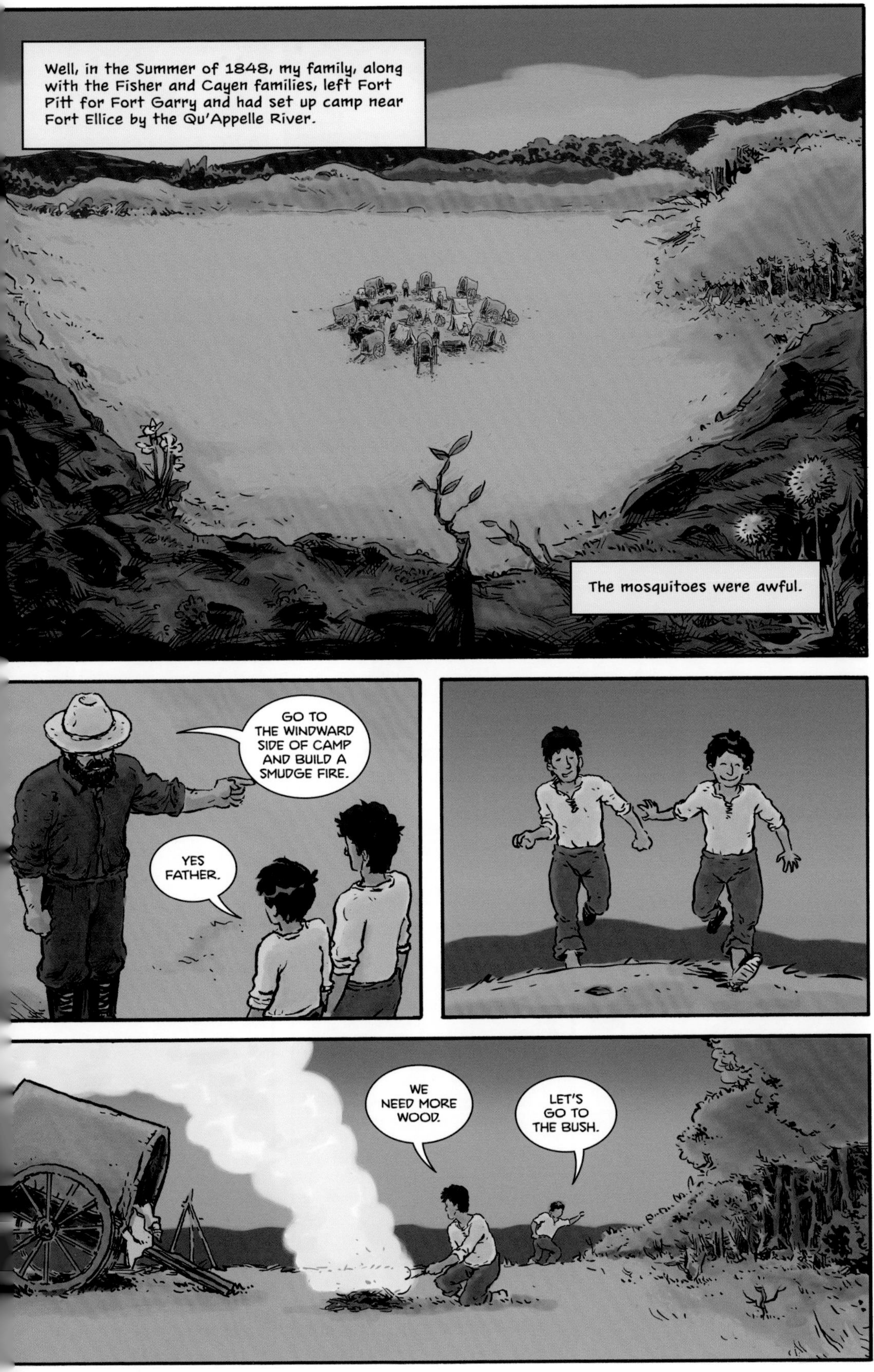
Well, in the Summer of 1848, my family, along with the Fisher and Cayen families, left Fort Pitt for Fort Garry and had set up camp near Fort Ellice by the Qu'Appelle River.
The mosquitoes were awful.
GO TO THE WINDWARD SIDE OF CAMP AND BUILD A SMUDGE FIRE.
YES FATHER.
WE NEED MORE WOOD.
LET'S GO TO THE BUSH.

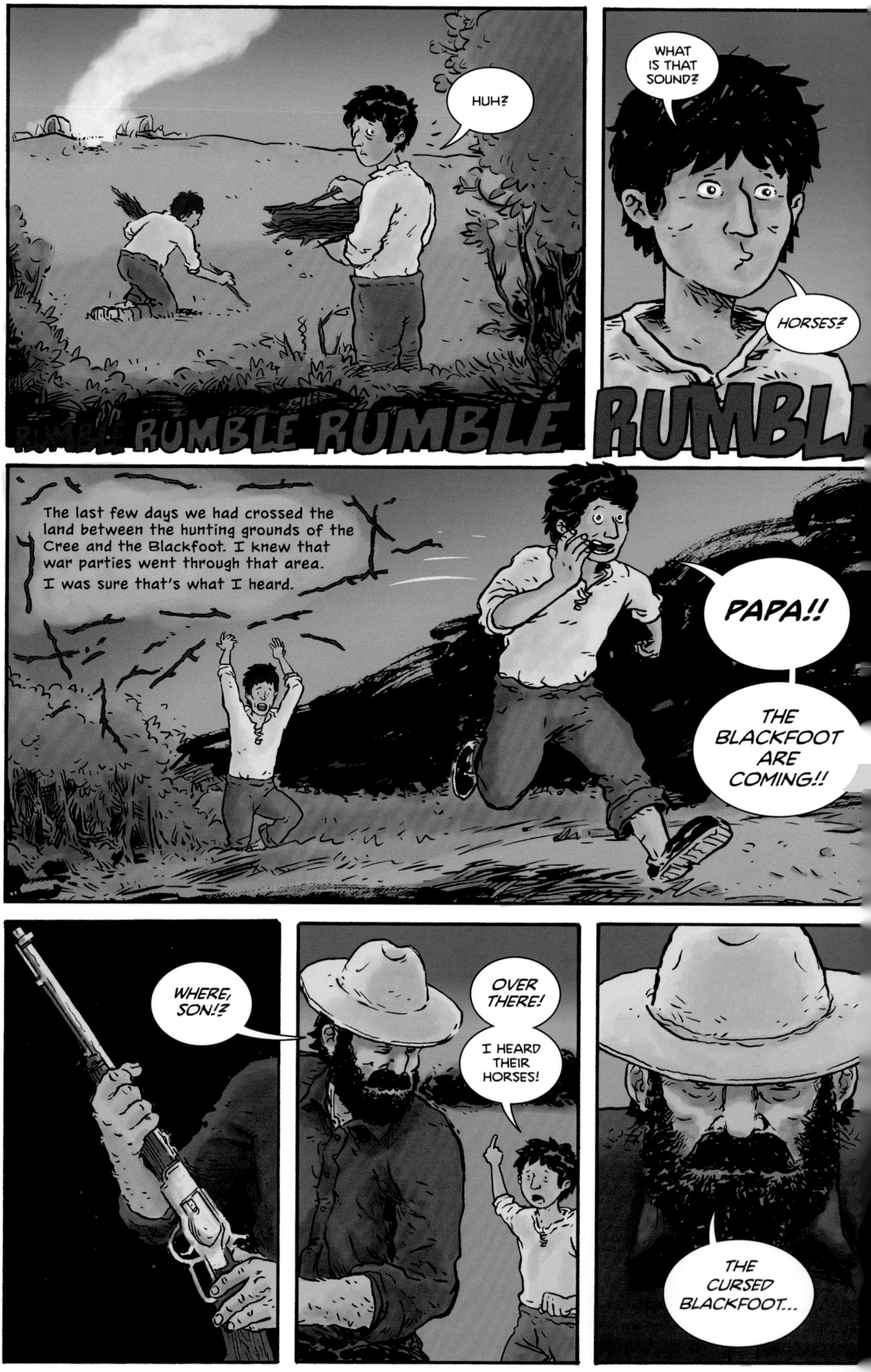
HUH?
WHAT IS THAT SOUND?
HORSES?
RUMBLE RUMBLE RUMBLE RUMBLE
The last few days we had crossed the land between the hunting grounds of the Cree and the Blackfoot. I knew that war parties went through that area.
I was sure that's what I heard.
PAPA!!
THE BLACKFOOT ARE COMING!!
WHERE, SON!?
OVER THERE!
I HEARD THEIR HORSES!
THE CURSED BLACKFOOT...

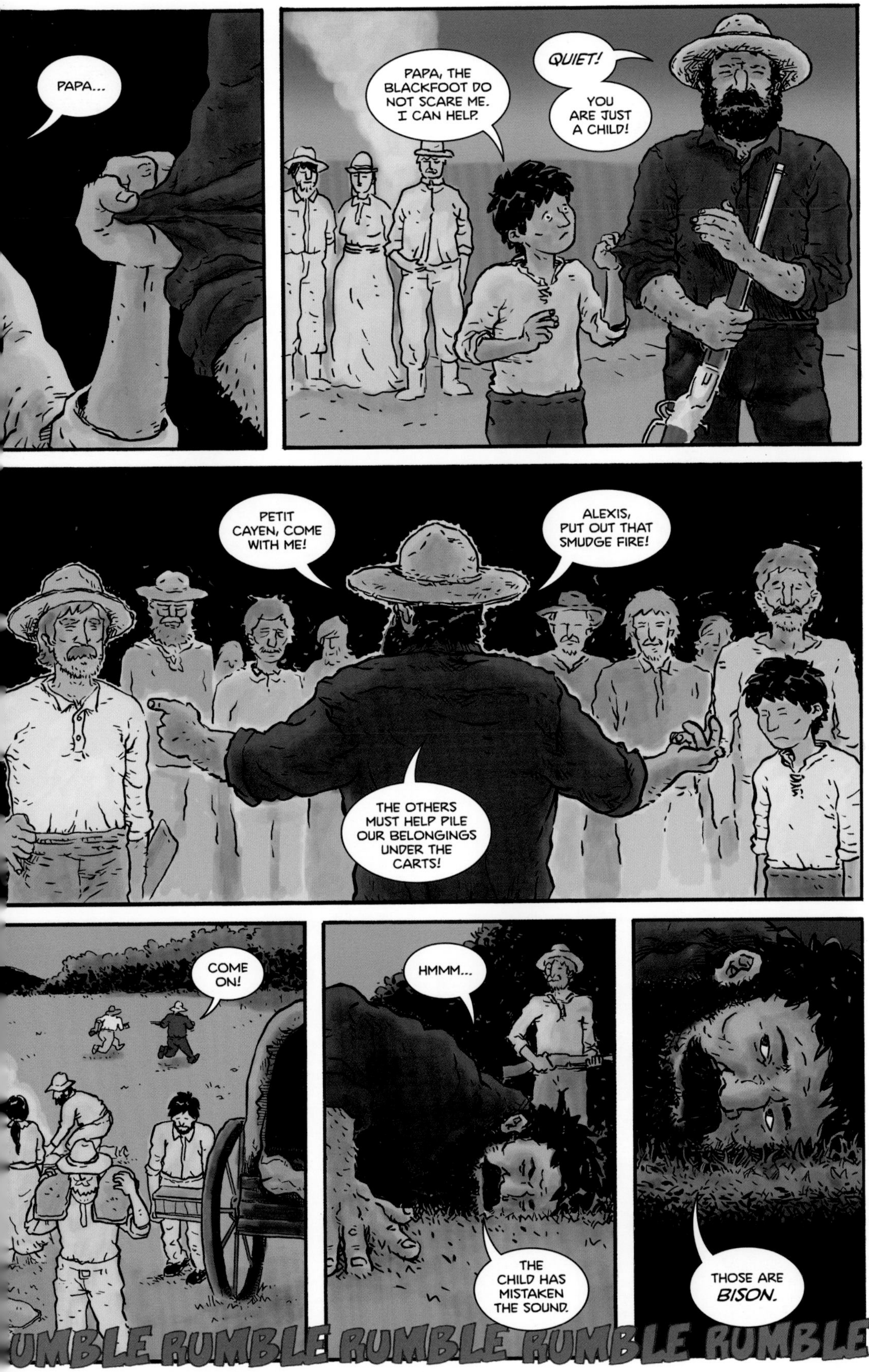
PAPA...
PAPA, THE BLACKFOOT DO NOT SCARE ME. I CAN HELP.
QUIET!
YOU ARE JUST A CHILD!
PETIT CAYEN, COME WITH ME!
ALEXIS, PUT OUT THAT SMUDGE FIRE!
THE OTHERS MUST HELP PILE OUR BELONGINGS UNDER THE CARTS!
COME ON!
HMMM...
THE CHILD HAS MISTAKEN THE SOUND.
THOSE ARE *BISON*.
UMBLE RUMBLE RUMBLE RUMBLE RUMBLE

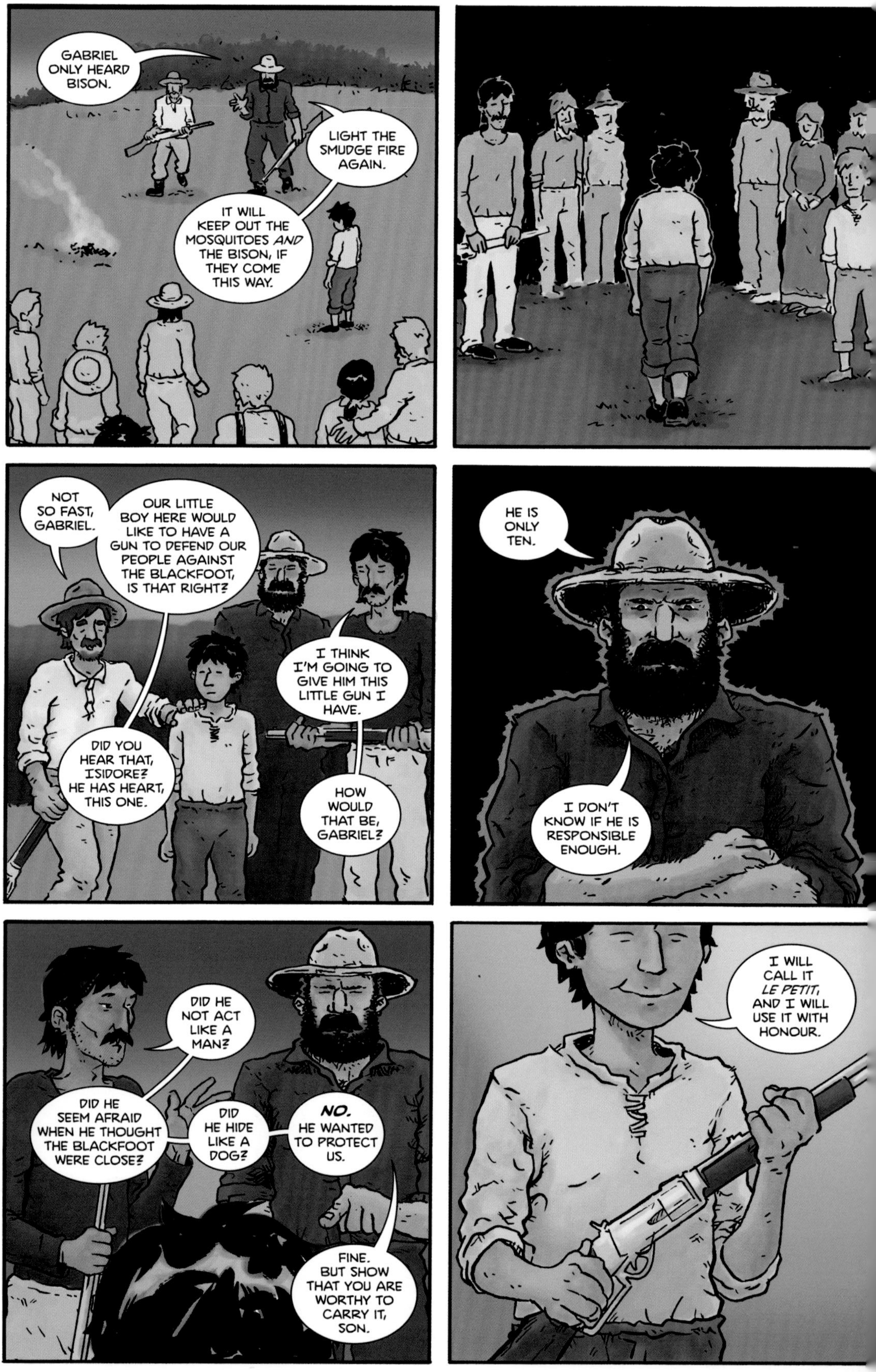
GABRIEL ONLY HEARD BISON.
LIGHT THE SMUDGE FIRE AGAIN.
IT WILL KEEP OUT THE MOSQUITOES *AND* THE BISON, IF THEY COME THIS WAY.
NOT SO FAST, GABRIEL.
OUR LITTLE BOY HERE WOULD LIKE TO HAVE A GUN TO DEFEND OUR PEOPLE AGAINST THE BLACKFOOT, IS THAT RIGHT?
DID YOU HEAR THAT, ISIDORE? HE HAS HEART, THIS ONE.
I THINK I'M GOING TO GIVE HIM THIS LITTLE GUN I HAVE.
HOW WOULD THAT BE, GABRIEL?
HE IS ONLY TEN.
I DON'T KNOW IF HE IS RESPONSIBLE ENOUGH.
DID HE NOT ACT LIKE A MAN?
DID HE SEEM AFRAID WHEN HE THOUGHT THE BLACKFOOT WERE CLOSE?
DID HE HIDE LIKE A DOG?
NO. HE WANTED TO PROTECT US.
FINE. BUT SHOW THAT YOU ARE WORTHY TO CARRY IT, SON.
I WILL CALL IT *LE PETIT*, AND I WILL USE IT WITH HONOUR.

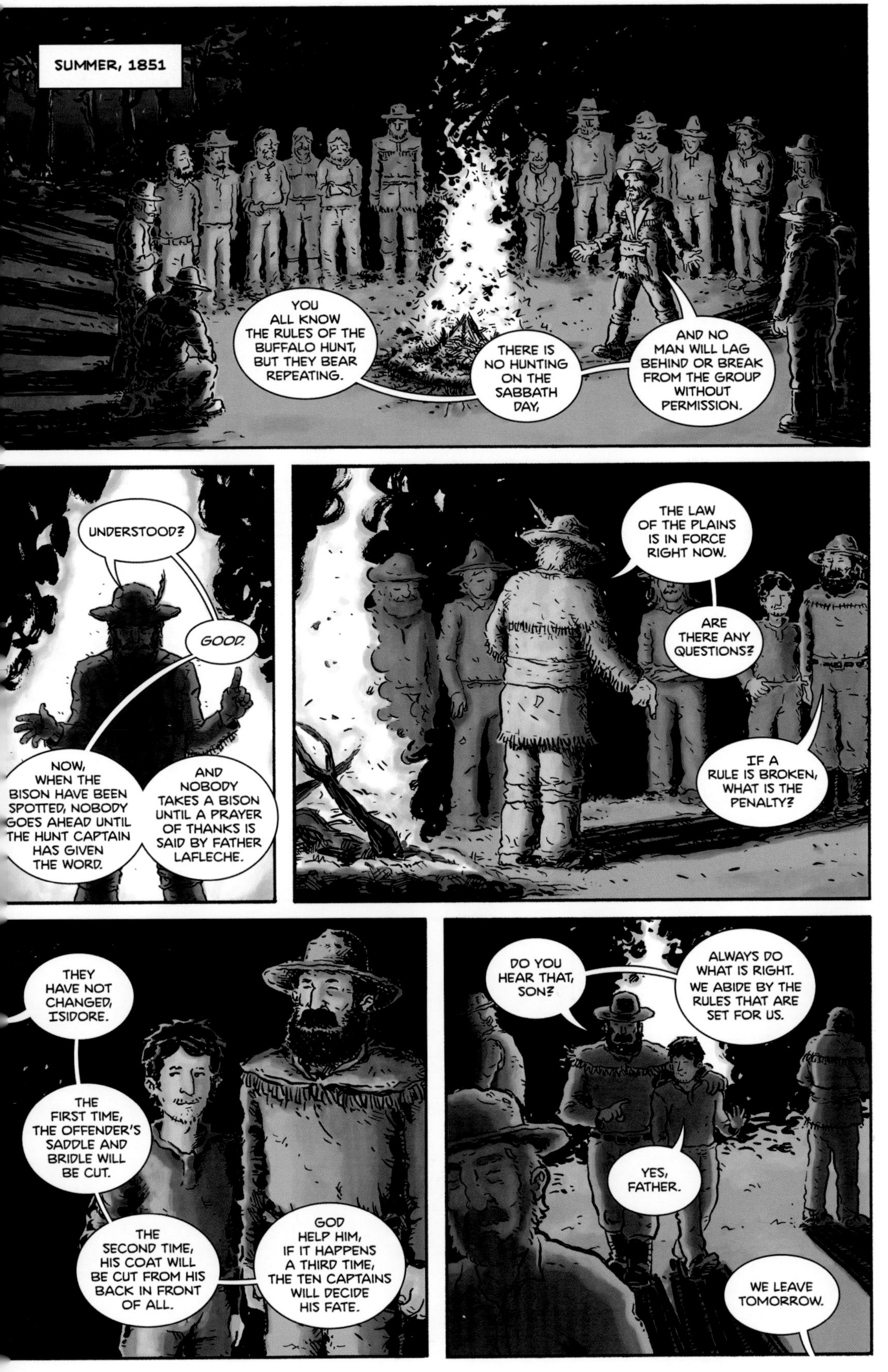
SUMMER, 1851
YOU ALL KNOW THE RULES OF THE BUFFALO HUNT, BUT THEY BEAR REPEATING.
THERE IS NO HUNTING ON THE SABBATH DAY,
AND NO MAN WILL LAG BEHIND OR BREAK FROM THE GROUP WITHOUT PERMISSION.
UNDERSTOOD?
GOOD.
NOW, WHEN THE BISON HAVE BEEN SPOTTED, NOBODY GOES AHEAD UNTIL THE HUNT CAPTAIN HAS GIVEN THE WORD.
AND NOBODY TAKES A BISON UNTIL A PRAYER OF THANKS IS SAID BY FATHER LAFLECHE.
THE LAW OF THE PLAINS IS IN FORCE RIGHT NOW.
ARE THERE ANY QUESTIONS?
IF A RULE IS BROKEN, WHAT IS THE PENALTY?
THEY HAVE NOT CHANGED, ISIDORE.
THE FIRST TIME, THE OFFENDER'S SADDLE AND BRIDLE WILL BE CUT.
THE SECOND TIME, HIS COAT WILL BE CUT FROM HIS BACK IN FRONT OF ALL.
GOD HELP HIM, IF IT HAPPENS A THIRD TIME, THE TEN CAPTAINS WILL DECIDE HIS FATE.
DO YOU HEAR THAT, SON?
ALWAYS DO WHAT IS RIGHT. WE ABIDE BY THE RULES THAT ARE SET FOR US.
YES, FATHER.
WE LEAVE TOMORROW.

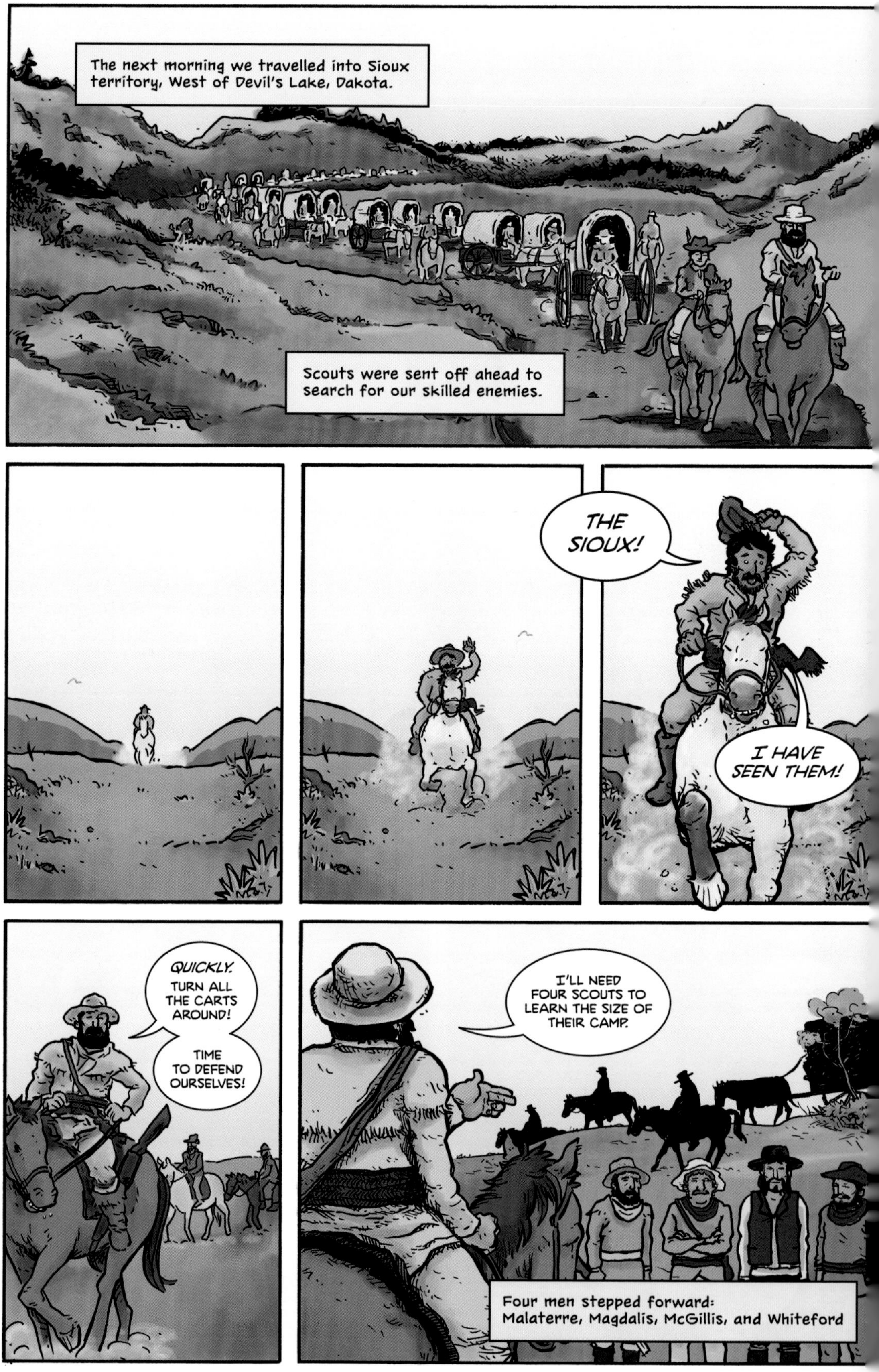

The next morning we travelled into Sioux territory, West of Devil's Lake, Dakota.
Scouts were sent off ahead to search for our skilled enemies.
THE SIOUX!
I HAVE SEEN THEM!
QUICKLY. TURN ALL THE CARTS AROUND!
TIME TO DEFEND OURSELVES!
I'LL NEED FOUR SCOUTS TO LEARN THE SIZE OF THEIR CAMP.
Four men stepped forward: Malaterre, Magdalis, McGillis, and Whiteford

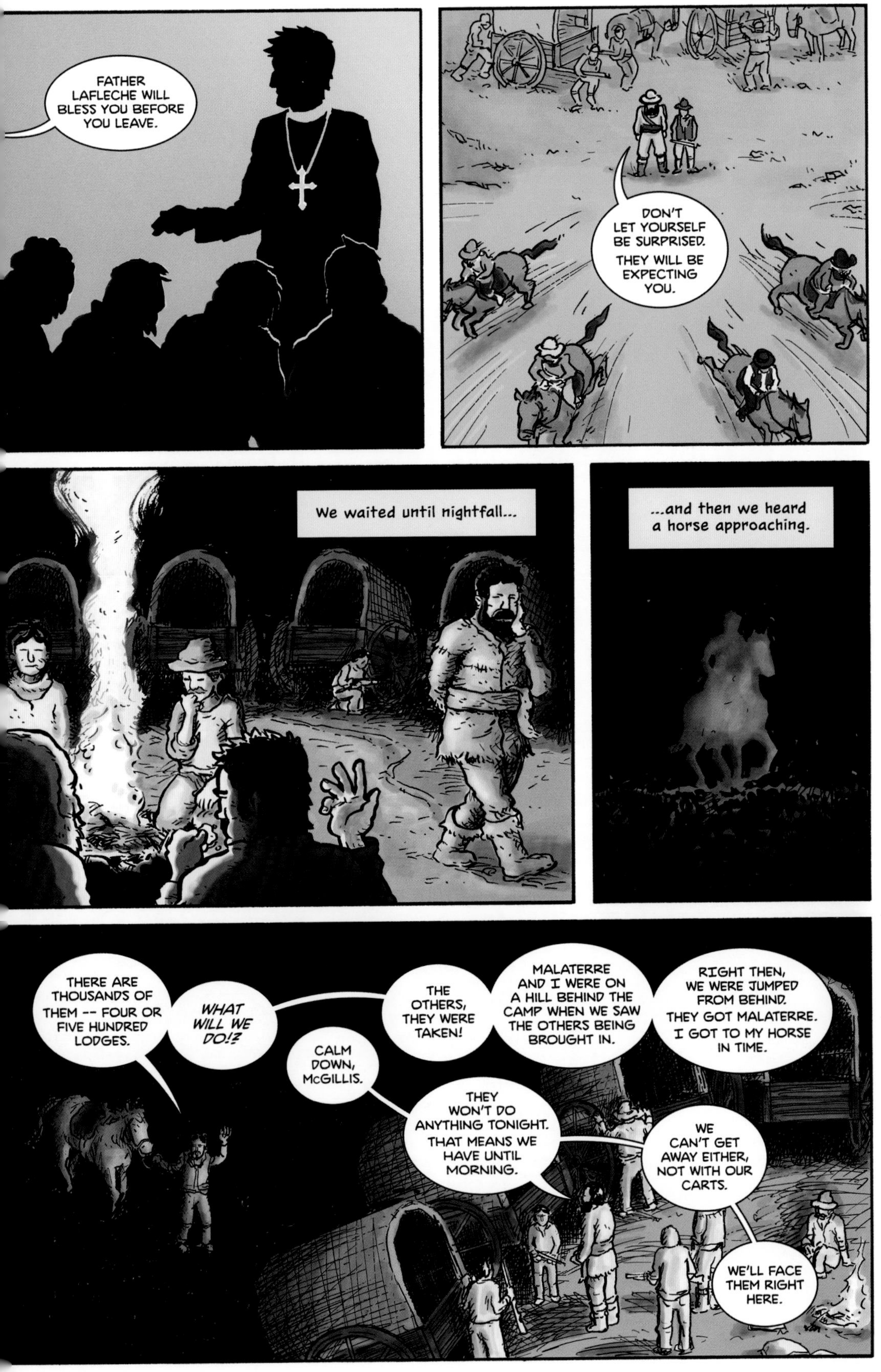
FATHER LAFLECHE WILL BLESS YOU BEFORE YOU LEAVE.
DON'T LET YOURSELF BE SURPRISED.
THEY WILL BE EXPECTING YOU.
We waited until nightfall...
...and then we heard a horse approaching.
THERE ARE THOUSANDS OF THEM -- FOUR OR FIVE HUNDRED LODGES.
WHAT WILL WE DO!?
THE OTHERS, THEY WERE TAKEN!
MALATERRE AND I WERE ON A HILL BEHIND THE CAMP WHEN WE SAW THE OTHERS BEING BROUGHT IN.
RIGHT THEN, WE WERE JUMPED FROM BEHIND.
THEY GOT MALATERRE. I GOT TO MY HORSE IN TIME.
CALM DOWN, McGILLIS.
THEY WON'T DO ANYTHING TONIGHT.
THAT MEANS WE HAVE UNTIL MORNING.
WE CAN'T GET AWAY EITHER, NOT WITH OUR CARTS.
WE'LL FACE THEM RIGHT HERE.

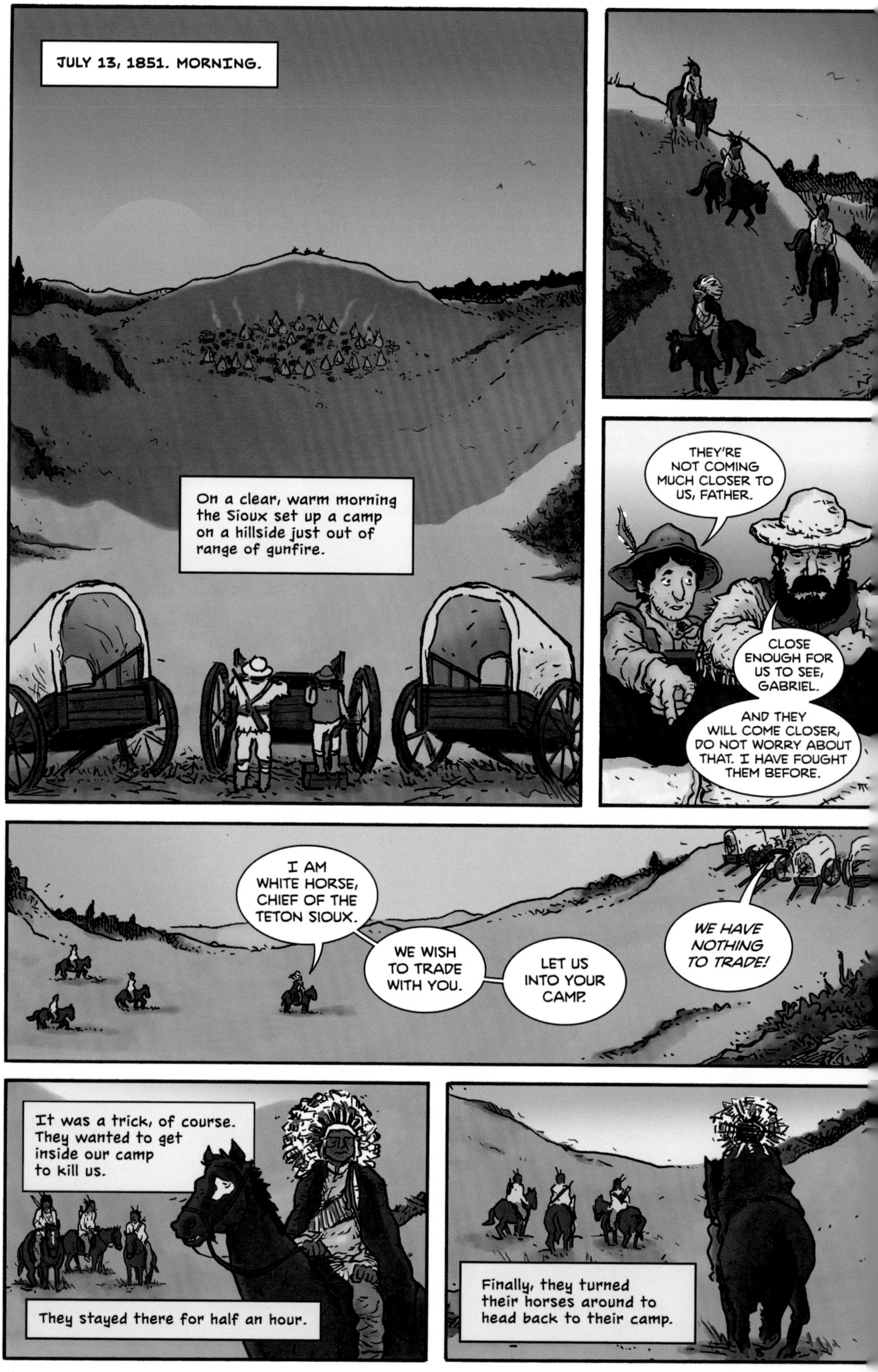

JULY 13, 1851. MORNING.
On a clear, warm morning the Sioux set up a camp on a hillside just out of range of gunfire.
THEY'RE NOT COMING MUCH CLOSER TO US, FATHER.
CLOSE ENOUGH FOR US TO SEE, GABRIEL.
AND THEY WILL COME CLOSER, DO NOT WORRY ABOUT THAT. I HAVE FOUGHT THEM BEFORE.
I AM WHITE HORSE, CHIEF OF THE TETON SIOUX.
WE WISH TO TRADE WITH YOU.
LET US INTO YOUR CAMP.
WE HAVE NOTHING TO TRADE!
It was a trick, of course. They wanted to get inside our camp to kill us.
They stayed there for half an hour.
Finally, they turned their horses around to head back to their camp.

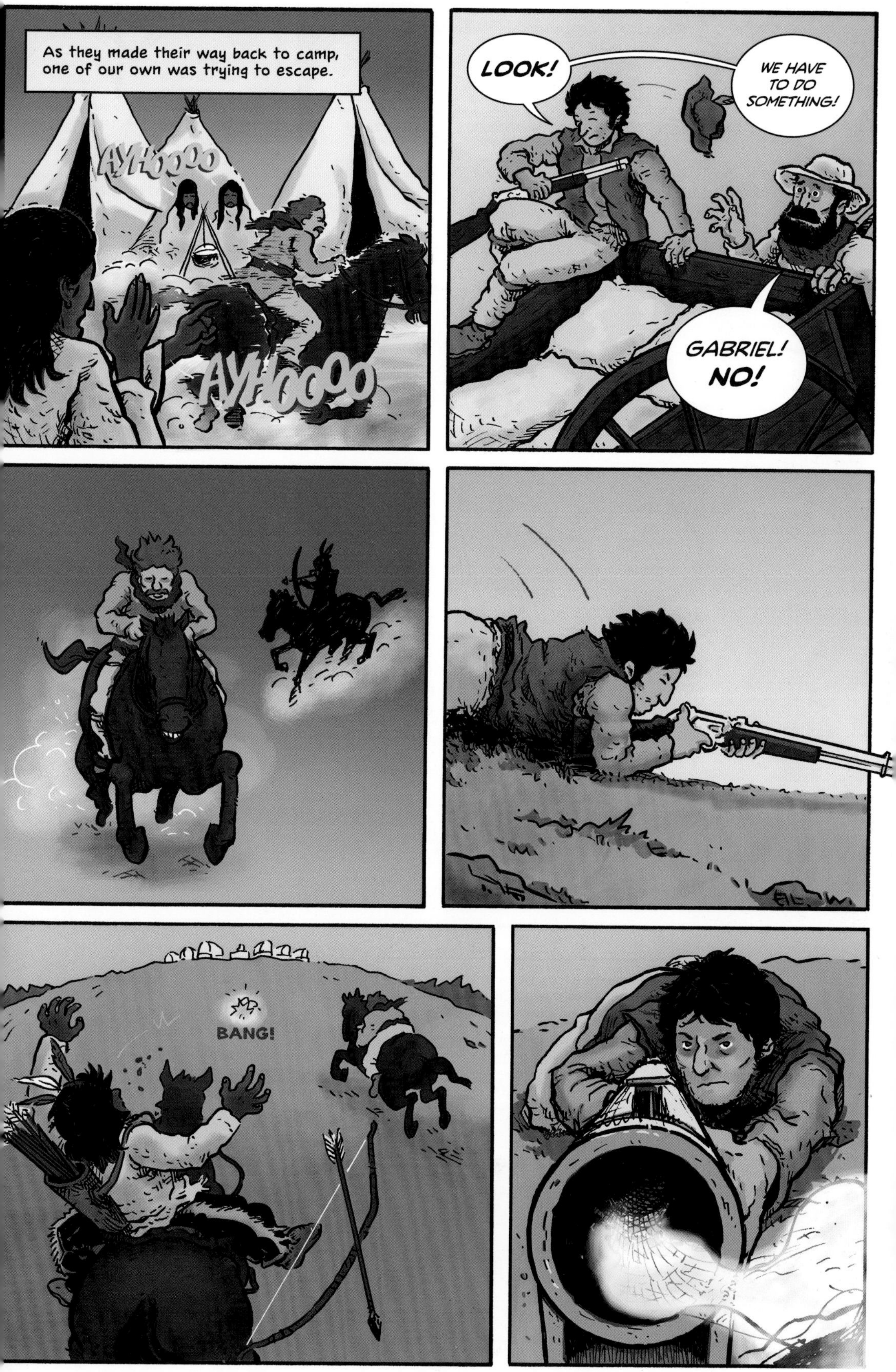
As they made their way back to camp, one of our own was trying to escape.
AYHOOOO
AYHOOOO
LOOK!
WE HAVE TO DO SOMETHING!
GABRIEL! NO!
BANG!

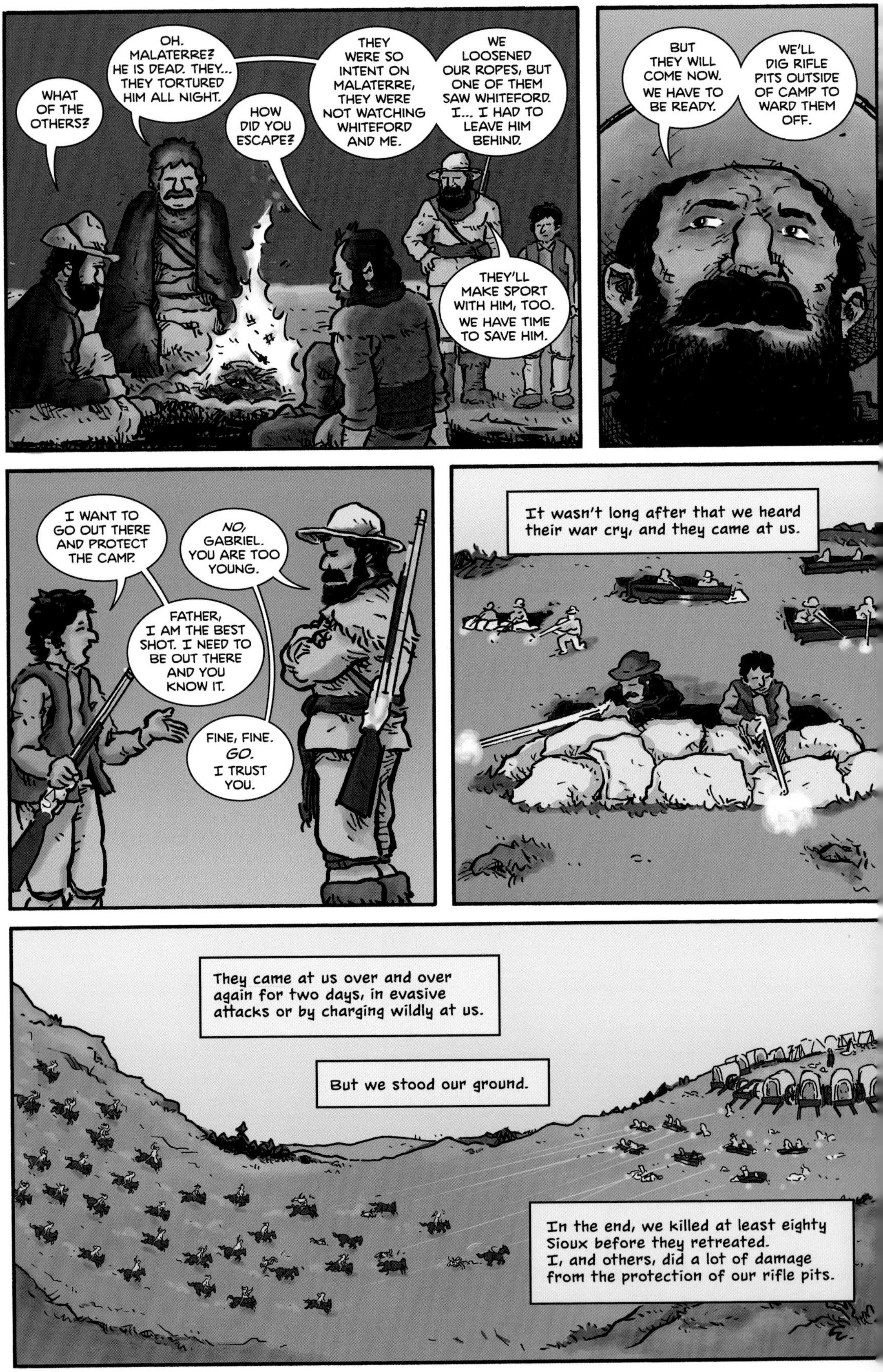
WHAT OF THE OTHERS?
OH. MALATERRE? HE IS DEAD. THEY... THEY TORTURED HIM ALL NIGHT.
HOW DID YOU ESCAPE?
THEY WERE SO INTENT ON MALATERRE, THEY WERE NOT WATCHING WHITEFORD AND ME.
WE LOOSENED OUR ROPES, BUT ONE OF THEM SAW WHITEFORD. I... I HAD TO LEAVE HIM BEHIND.
THEY'LL MAKE SPORT WITH HIM, TOO. WE HAVE TIME TO SAVE HIM.
BUT THEY WILL COME NOW. WE HAVE TO BE READY.
WE'LL DIG RIFLE PITS OUTSIDE OF CAMP TO WARD THEM OFF.
I WANT TO GO OUT THERE AND PROTECT THE CAMP.
NO, GABRIEL. YOU ARE TOO YOUNG.
FATHER, I AM THE BEST SHOT. I NEED TO BE OUT THERE AND YOU KNOW IT.
FINE, FINE. GO. I TRUST YOU.
It wasn't long after that we heard their war cry, and they came at us.
They came at us over and over again for two days, in evasive attacks or by charging wildly at us.
But we stood our ground.
In the end, we killed at least eighty Sioux before they retreated.
I, and others, did a lot of damage from the protection of our rifle pits.

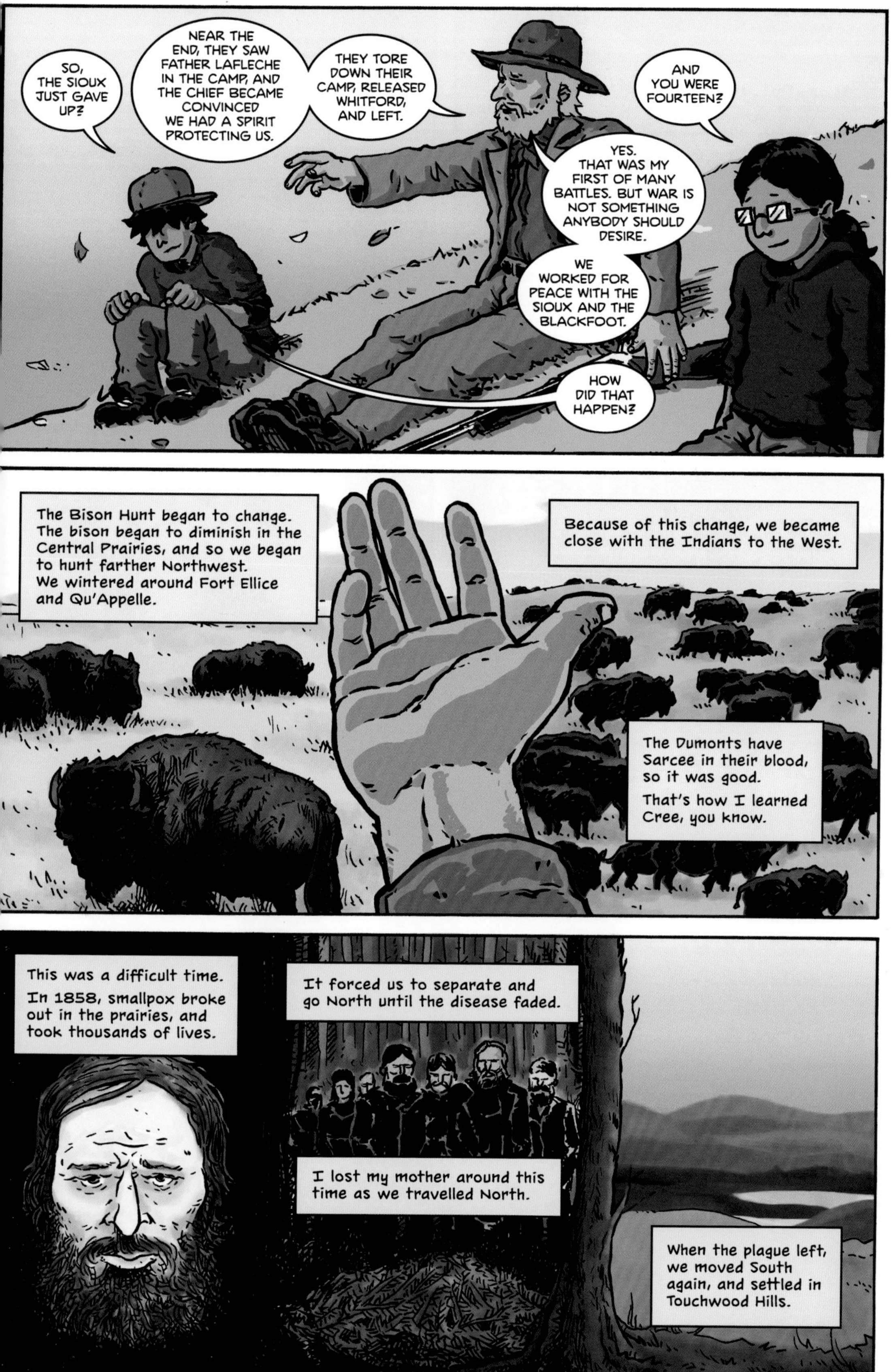
SO, THE SIOUX JUST GAVE UP?
NEAR THE END, THEY SAW FATHER LAFLECHE IN THE CAMP, AND THE CHIEF BECAME CONVINCED WE HAD A SPIRIT PROTECTING US.
THEY TORE DOWN THEIR CAMP, RELEASED WHITFORD, AND LEFT.
AND YOU WERE FOURTEEN?
YES. THAT WAS MY FIRST OF MANY BATTLES. BUT WAR IS NOT SOMETHING ANYBODY SHOULD DESIRE.
WE WORKED FOR PEACE WITH THE SIOUX AND THE BLACKFOOT.
HOW DID THAT HAPPEN?
The Bison Hunt began to change. The bison began to diminish in the Central Prairies, and so we began to hunt farther Northwest. We wintered around Fort Ellice and Qu'Appelle.
Because of this change, we became close with the Indians to the West.
The Dumonts have Sarcee in their blood, so it was good.
That's how I learned Cree, you know.
This was a difficult time.
In 1858, smallpox broke out in the prairies, and took thousands of lives.
It forced us to separate and go North until the disease faded.
I lost my mother around this time as we travelled North.
When the plague left, we moved South again, and settled in Touchwood Hills.

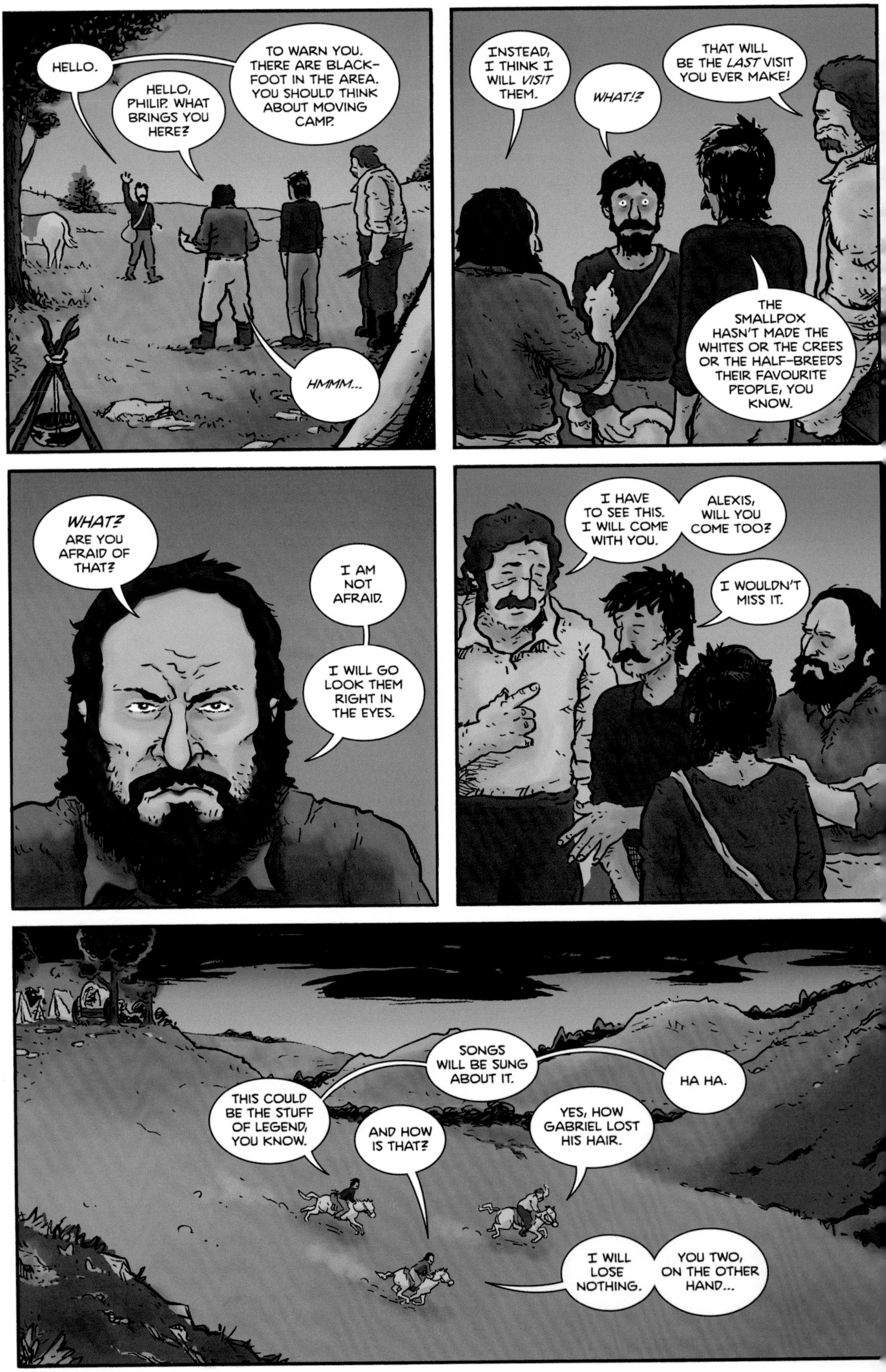
HELLO.
HELLO, PHILIP. WHAT BRINGS YOU HERE?
TO WARN YOU. THERE ARE BLACK-FOOT IN THE AREA. YOU SHOULD THINK ABOUT MOVING CAMP.
HMMM...
INSTEAD, I THINK I WILL VISIT THEM.
WHAT!?
THAT WILL BE THE LAST VISIT YOU EVER MAKE!
THE SMALLPOX HASN'T MADE THE WHITES OR THE CREES OR THE HALF-BREEDS THEIR FAVOURITE PEOPLE, YOU KNOW.
WHAT? ARE YOU AFRAID OF THAT?
I AM NOT AFRAID.
I WILL GO LOOK THEM RIGHT IN THE EYES.
I HAVE TO SEE THIS. I WILL COME WITH YOU.
ALEXIS, WILL YOU COME TOO?
I WOULDN'T MISS IT.
THIS COULD BE THE STUFF OF LEGEND, YOU KNOW.
AND HOW IS THAT?
SONGS WILL BE SUNG ABOUT IT.
HA HA.
YES, HOW GABRIEL LOST HIS HAIR.
I WILL LOSE NOTHING.
YOU TWO, ON THE OTHER HAND...

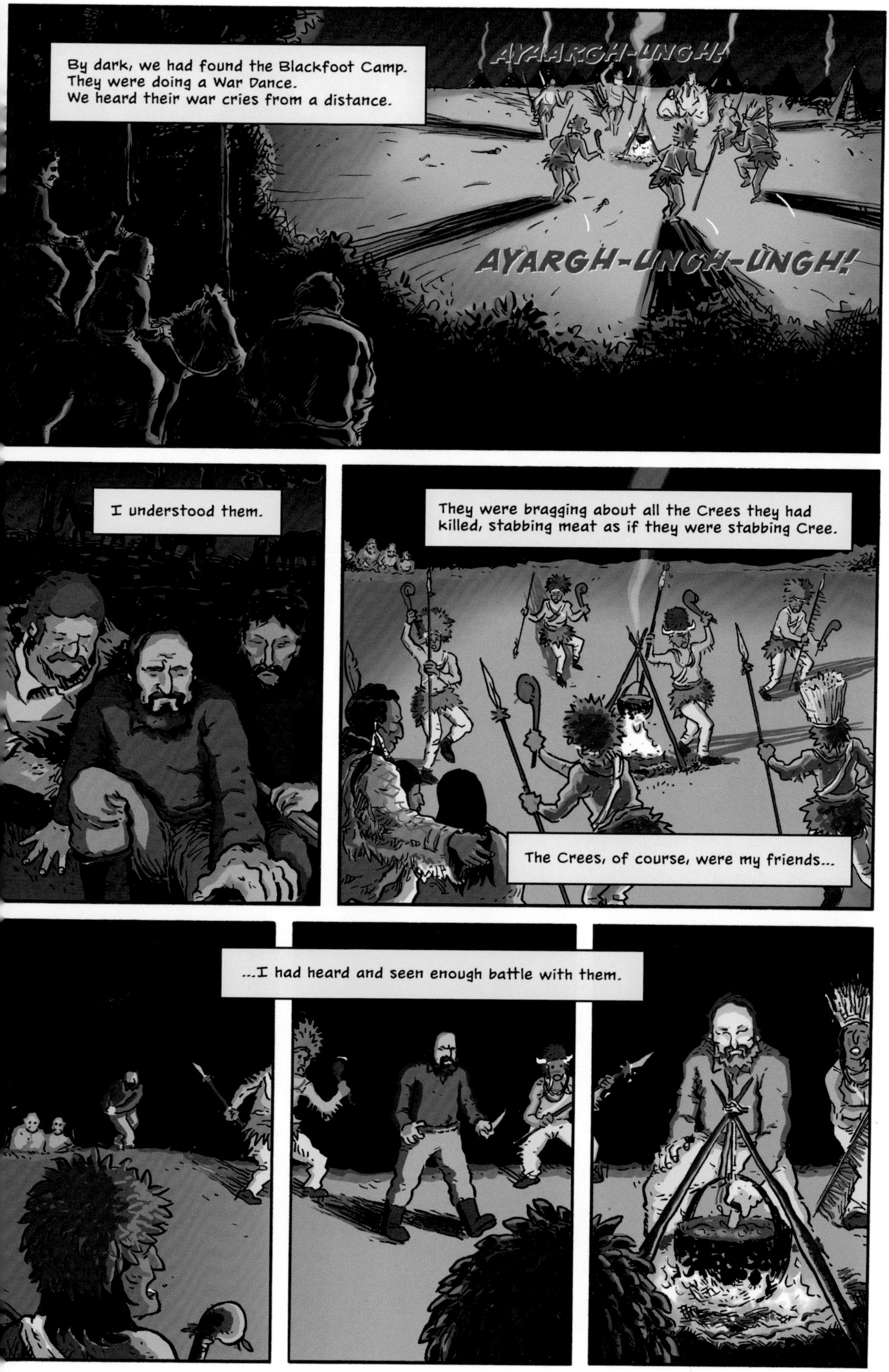
By dark, we had found the Blackfoot Camp.
They were doing a War Dance.
We heard their war cries from a distance.
AYAARGH-UNGH!
AYARGH-UNGH-UNGH!
I understood them.
They were bragging about all the Crees they had killed, stabbing meat as if they were stabbing Cree.
The Crees, of course, were my friends...
...I had heard and seen enough battle with them.

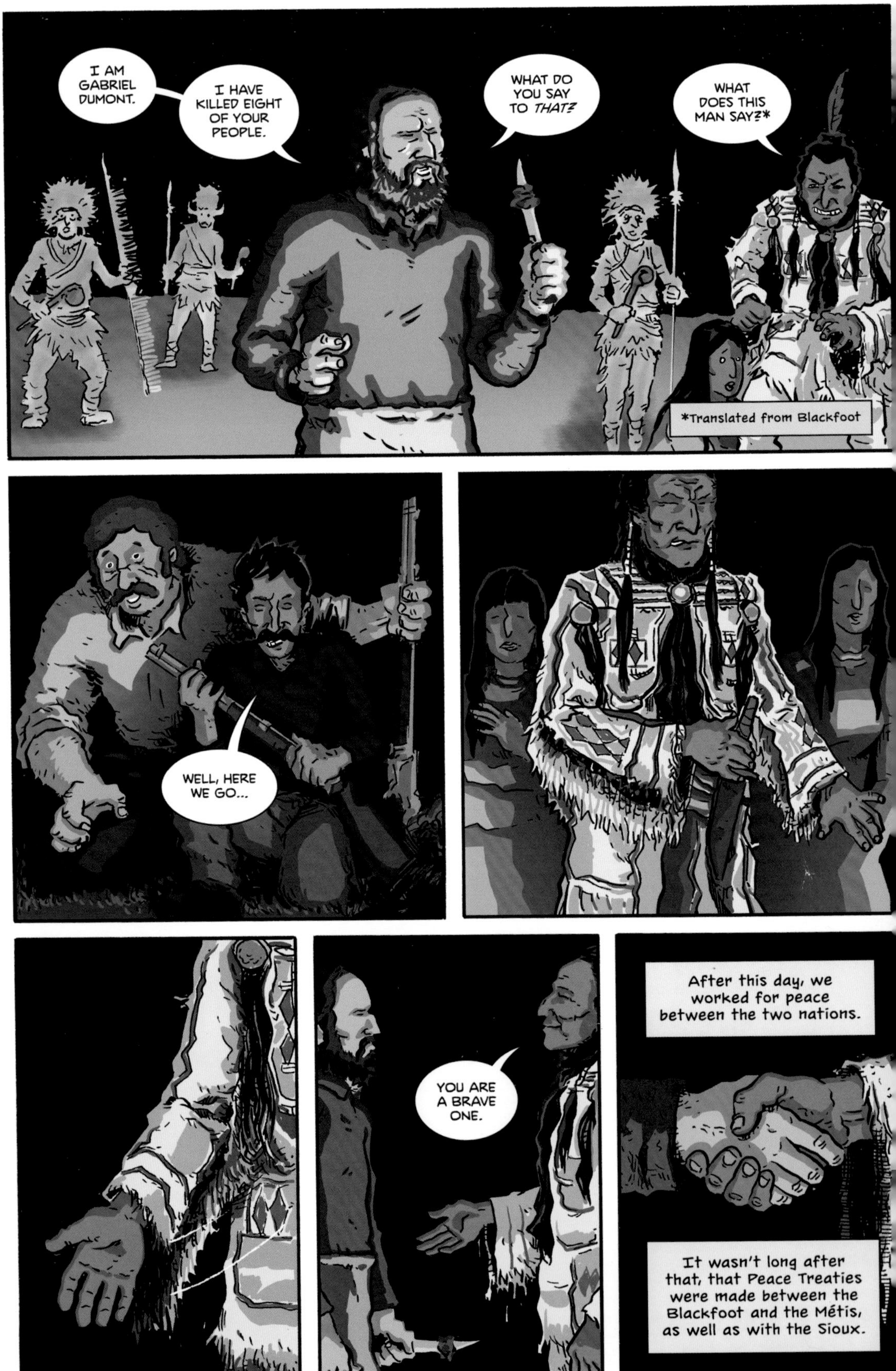

I AM GABRIEL DUMONT.
I HAVE KILLED EIGHT OF YOUR PEOPLE.
WHAT DO YOU SAY TO *THAT?*
WHAT DOES THIS MAN SAY?*
*Translated from Blackfoot
WELL, HERE WE GO...
YOU ARE A BRAVE ONE.
After this day, we worked for peace between the two nations.
It wasn't long after that, that Peace Treaties were made between the Blackfoot and the Métis, as well as with the Sioux.

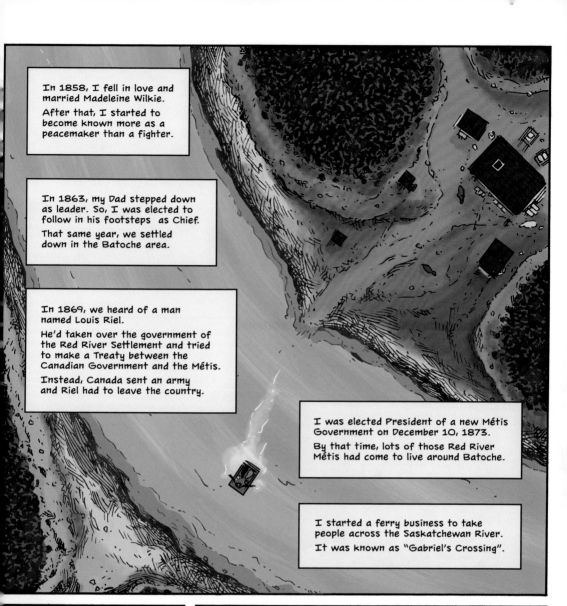

In 1858, I fell in love and married Madeleine Wilkie.

After that, I started to become known more as a peacemaker than a fighter.

In 1863, my Dad stepped down as leader. So, I was elected to follow in his footsteps as Chief.

That same year, we settled down in the Batoche area.

In 1869, we heard of a man named Louis Riel.

He'd taken over the government of the Red River Settlement and tried to make a Treaty between the Canadian Government and the Métis.

Instead, Canada sent an army and Riel had to leave the country.

I was elected President of a new Métis Government on December 10, 1873.

By that time, lots of those Red River Métis had come to live around Batoche.

I started a ferry business to take people across the Saskatchewan River.

It was known as "Gabriel's Crossing".

NOTICE.

Gabriel's Crossing.

The public are informed that GABRIEL'S Crossing is now in readiness for the accommodation of the public.

One Scow, the Best on the River,

will be in constant readiness. The road by this ferry is the SHORTEST by twenty-five miles going to or going east from Battleford.

The public promptly attended to.

GABRIEL DUMONT.

May, 1880.

Of course, the Whites were moving West, too.

Surveyors came across the land, marking it for future settlement. We had to go and claim the land we already lived on. We all got really upset about that, and in 1884 we decided to do something about it.

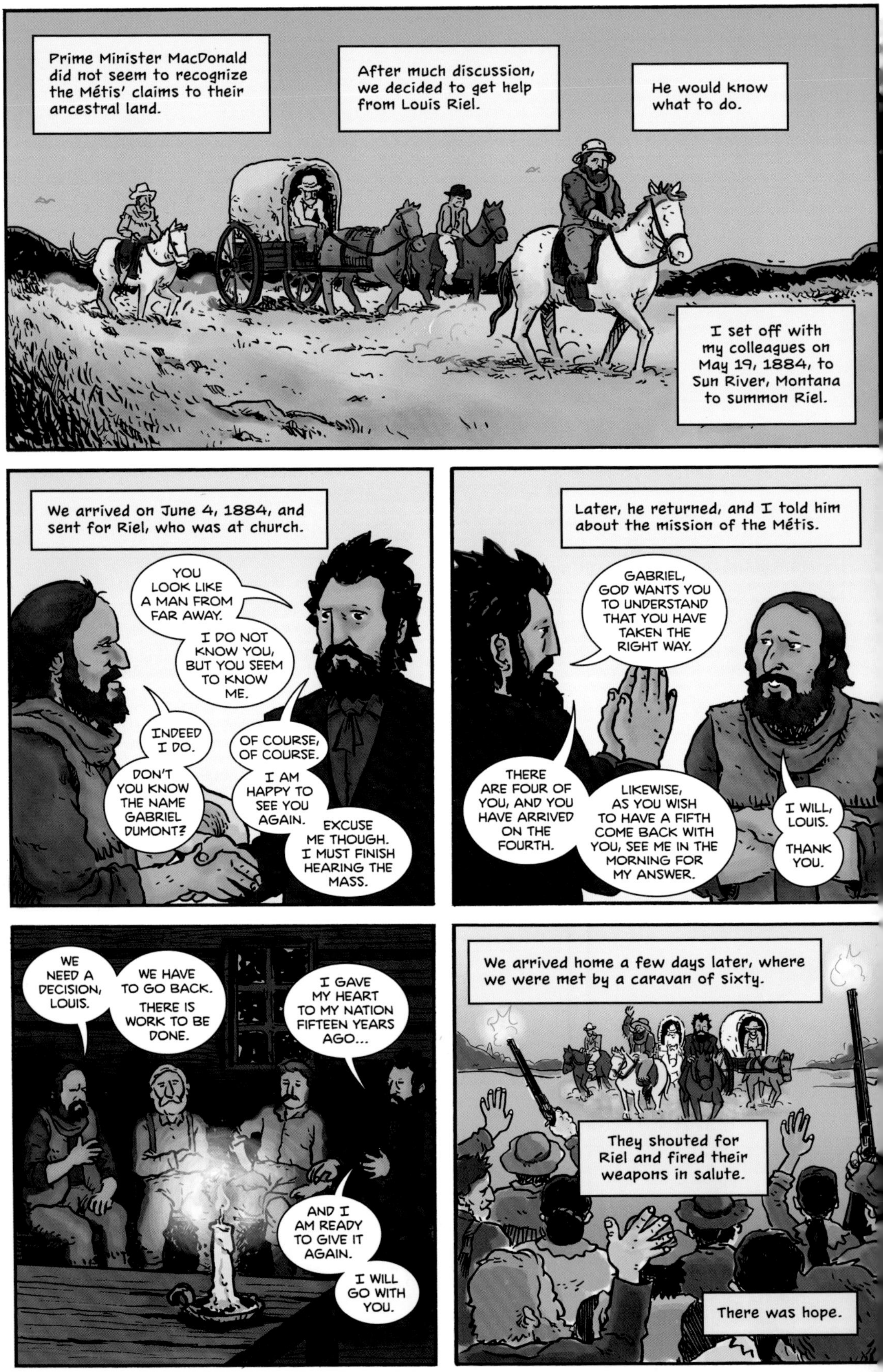
Prime Minister MacDonald did not seem to recognize the Métis' claims to their ancestral land.
After much discussion, we decided to get help from Louis Riel.
He would know what to do.
I set off with my colleagues on May 19, 1884, to Sun River, Montana to summon Riel.
We arrived on June 4, 1884, and sent for Riel, who was at church.
YOU LOOK LIKE A MAN FROM FAR AWAY.
I DO NOT KNOW YOU, BUT YOU SEEM TO KNOW ME.
INDEED I DO.
DON'T YOU KNOW THE NAME GABRIEL DUMONT?
OF COURSE, OF COURSE.
I AM HAPPY TO SEE YOU AGAIN.
EXCUSE ME THOUGH. I MUST FINISH HEARING THE MASS.
Later, he returned, and I told him about the mission of the Métis.
GABRIEL, GOD WANTS YOU TO UNDERSTAND THAT YOU HAVE TAKEN THE RIGHT WAY.
THERE ARE FOUR OF YOU, AND YOU HAVE ARRIVED ON THE FOURTH.
LIKEWISE, AS YOU WISH TO HAVE A FIFTH COME BACK WITH YOU, SEE ME IN THE MORNING FOR MY ANSWER.
I WILL, LOUIS.
THANK YOU.
WE NEED A DECISION, LOUIS.
WE HAVE TO GO BACK.
THERE IS WORK TO BE DONE.
I GAVE MY HEART TO MY NATION FIFTEEN YEARS AGO...
AND I AM READY TO GIVE IT AGAIN.
I WILL GO WITH YOU.
We arrived home a few days later, where we were met by a caravan of sixty.
They shouted for Riel and fired their weapons in salute.
There was hope.

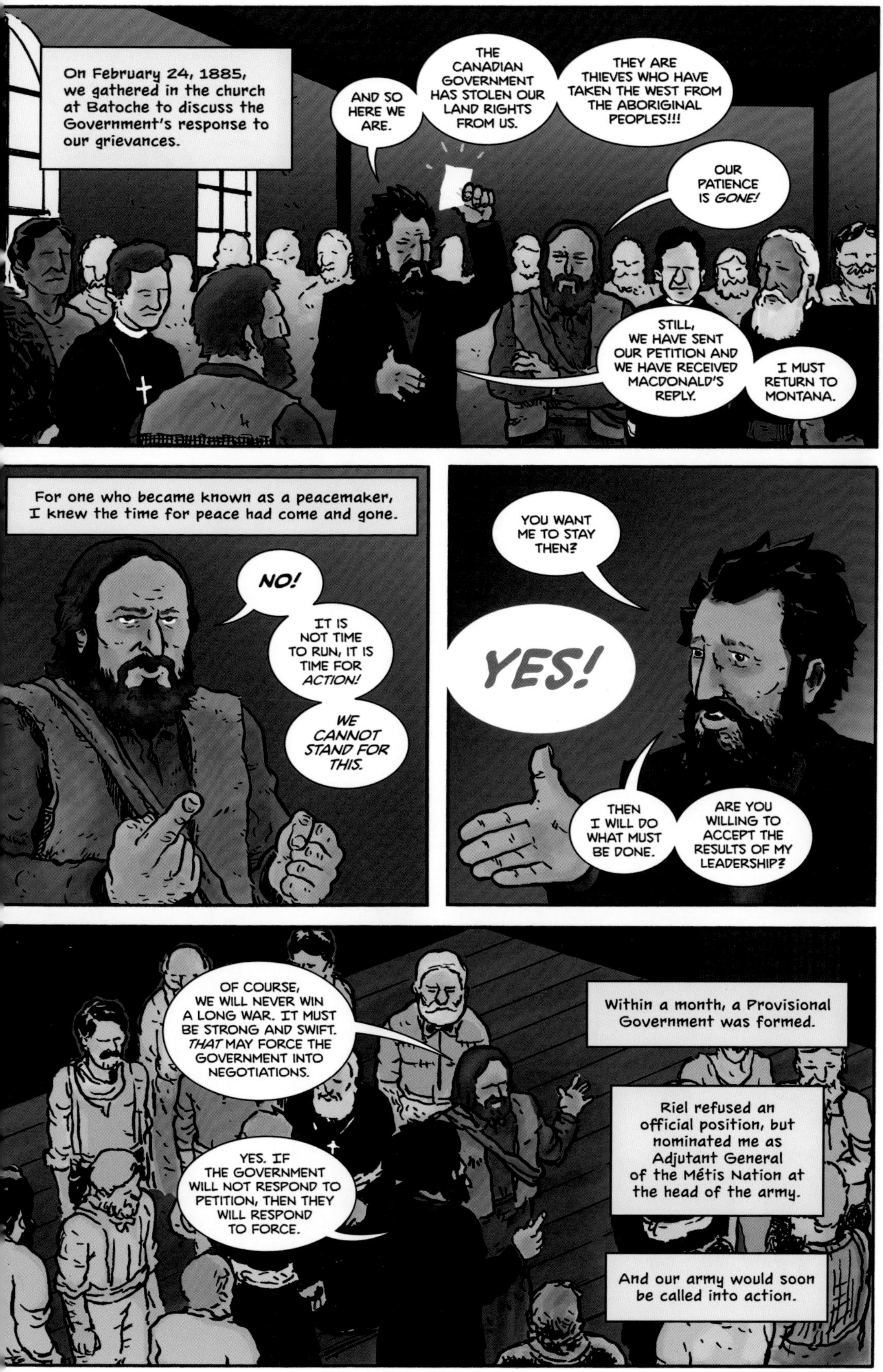
On February 24, 1885, we gathered in the church at Batoche to discuss the Government's response to our grievances.
AND SO HERE WE ARE.
THE CANADIAN GOVERNMENT HAS STOLEN OUR LAND RIGHTS FROM US.
THEY ARE THIEVES WHO HAVE TAKEN THE WEST FROM THE ABORIGINAL PEOPLES!!!
OUR PATIENCE IS *GONE!*
STILL, WE HAVE SENT OUR PETITION AND WE HAVE RECEIVED MACDONALD'S REPLY.
I MUST RETURN TO MONTANA.
For one who became known as a peacemaker, I knew the time for peace had come and gone.
NO!
IT IS NOT TIME TO RUN, IT IS TIME FOR *ACTION!*
WE CANNOT STAND FOR THIS.
YOU WANT ME TO STAY THEN?
YES!
THEN I WILL DO WHAT MUST BE DONE.
ARE YOU WILLING TO ACCEPT THE RESULTS OF MY LEADERSHIP?
OF COURSE, WE WILL NEVER WIN A LONG WAR. IT MUST BE STRONG AND SWIFT. *THAT* MAY FORCE THE GOVERNMENT INTO NEGOTIATIONS.
YES. IF THE GOVERNMENT WILL NOT RESPOND TO PETITION, THEN THEY WILL RESPOND TO FORCE.
Within a month, a Provisional Government was formed.
Riel refused an official position, but nominated me as Adjutant General of the Métis Nation at the head of the army.
And our army would soon be called into action.

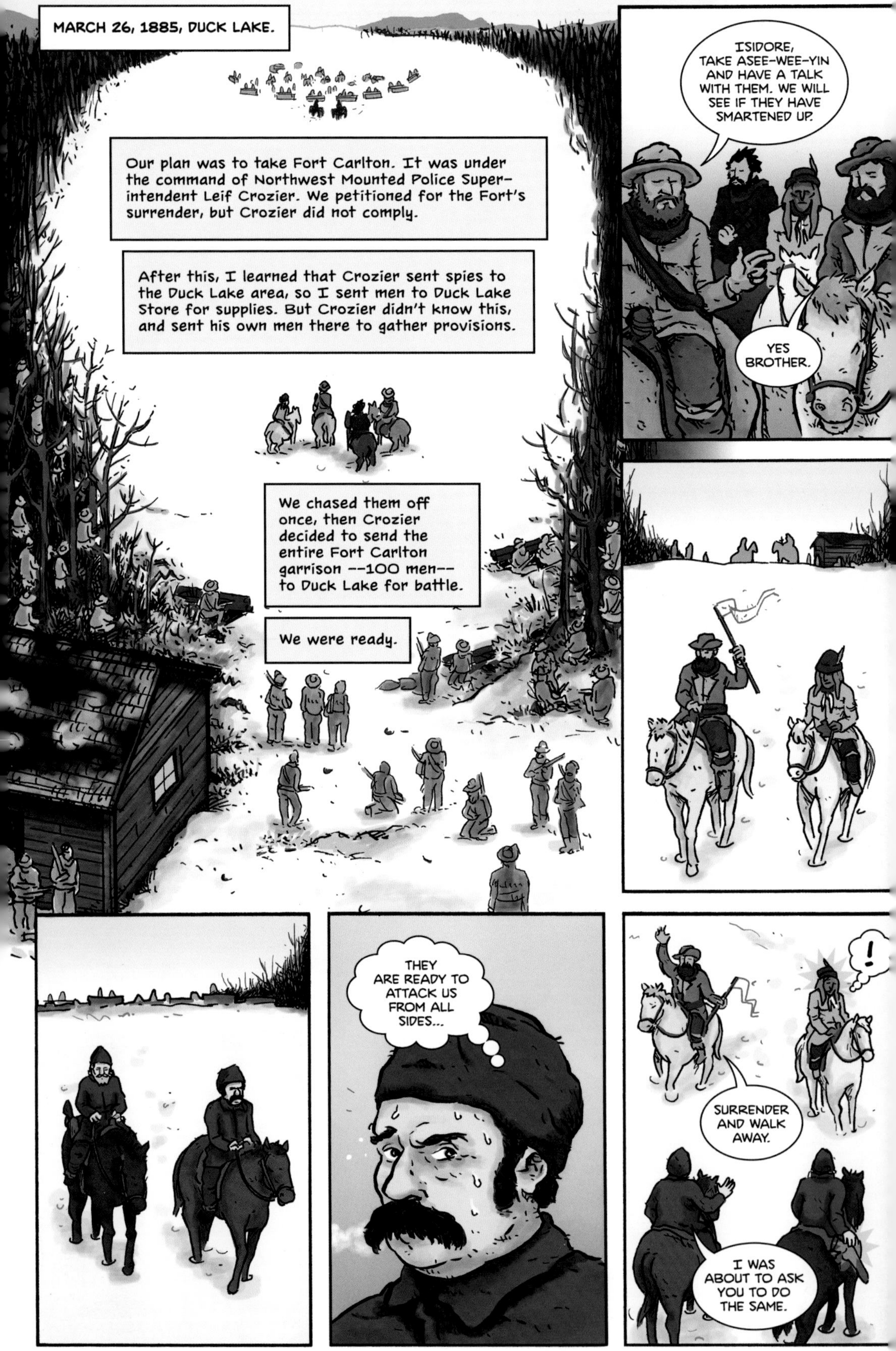

MARCH 26, 1885, DUCK LAKE.
Our plan was to take Fort Carlton. It was under the command of Northwest Mounted Police Superintendent Leif Crozier. We petitioned for the Fort's surrender, but Crozier did not comply.
After this, I learned that Crozier sent spies to the Duck Lake area, so I sent men to Duck Lake Store for supplies. But Crozier didn't know this, and sent his own men there to gather provisions.
We chased them off once, then Crozier decided to send the entire Fort Carlton garrison --100 men-- to Duck Lake for battle.
We were ready.
ISIDORE, TAKE ASEE-WEE-YIN AND HAVE A TALK WITH THEM. WE WILL SEE IF THEY HAVE SMARTENED UP.
YES BROTHER.
THEY ARE READY TO ATTACK US FROM ALL SIDES...
!
SURRENDER AND WALK AWAY.
I WAS ABOUT TO ASK YOU TO DO THE SAME.

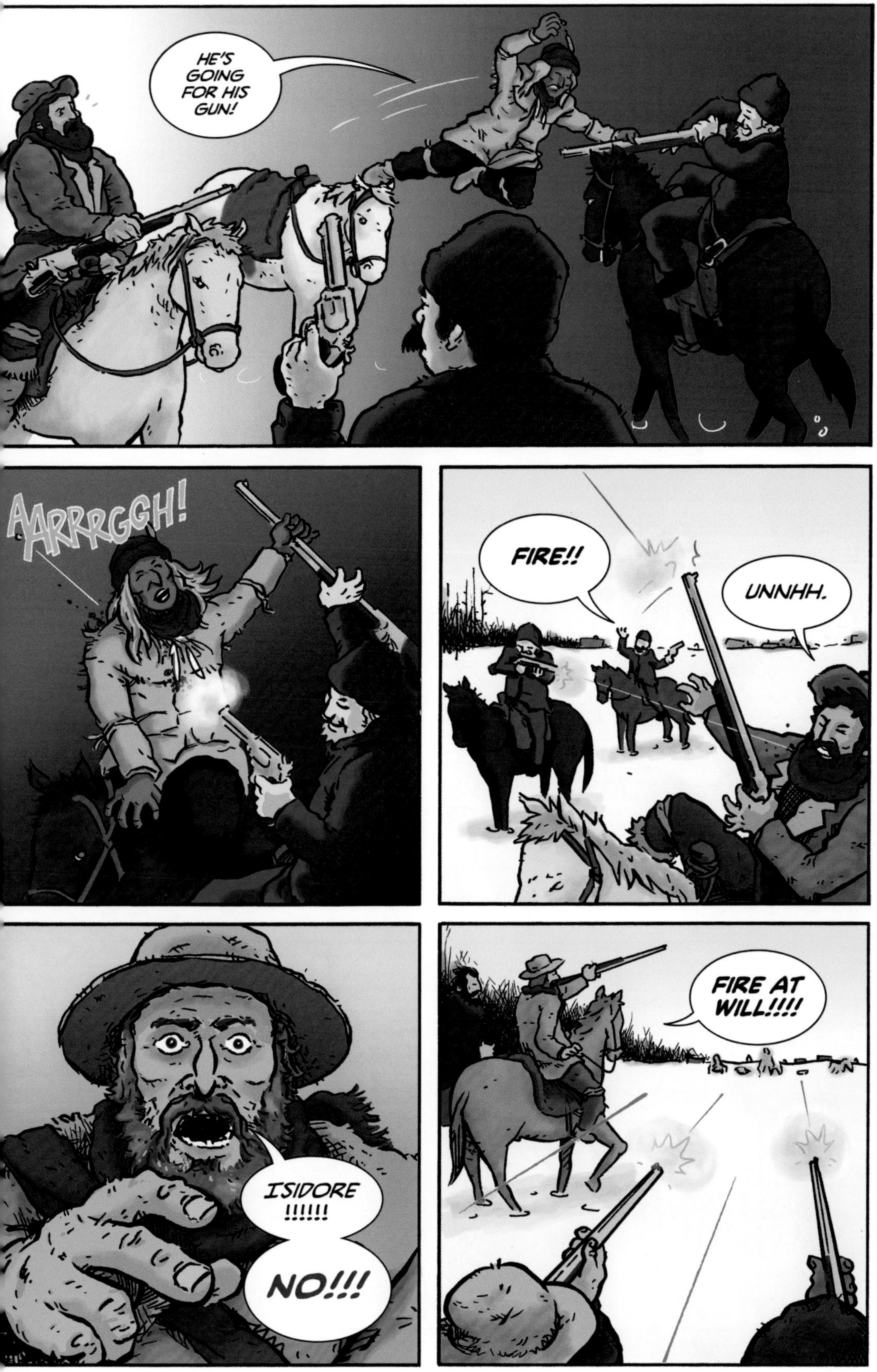
HE'S GOING FOR HIS GUN!
AARRRGGH!
FIRE!!
UNNHH.
ISIDORE !!!!!!
NO!!!
FIRE AT WILL!!!!

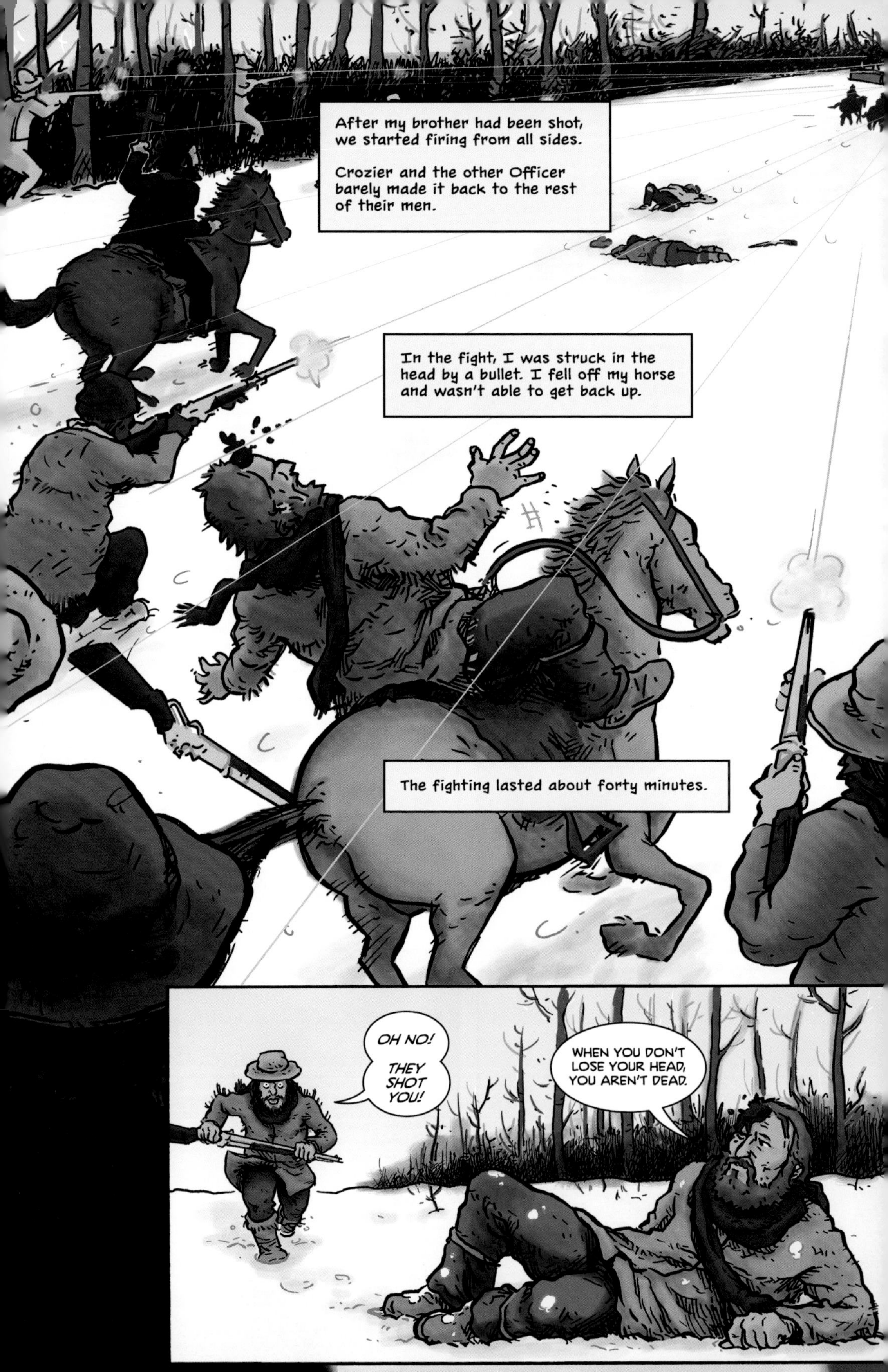

After my brother had been shot, we started firing from all sides.
Crozier and the other Officer barely made it back to the rest of their men.
In the fight, I was struck in the head by a bullet. I fell off my horse and wasn't able to get back up.
The fighting lasted about forty minutes.
OH NO! THEY SHOT YOU!
WHEN YOU DON'T LOSE YOUR HEAD, YOU AREN'T DEAD.

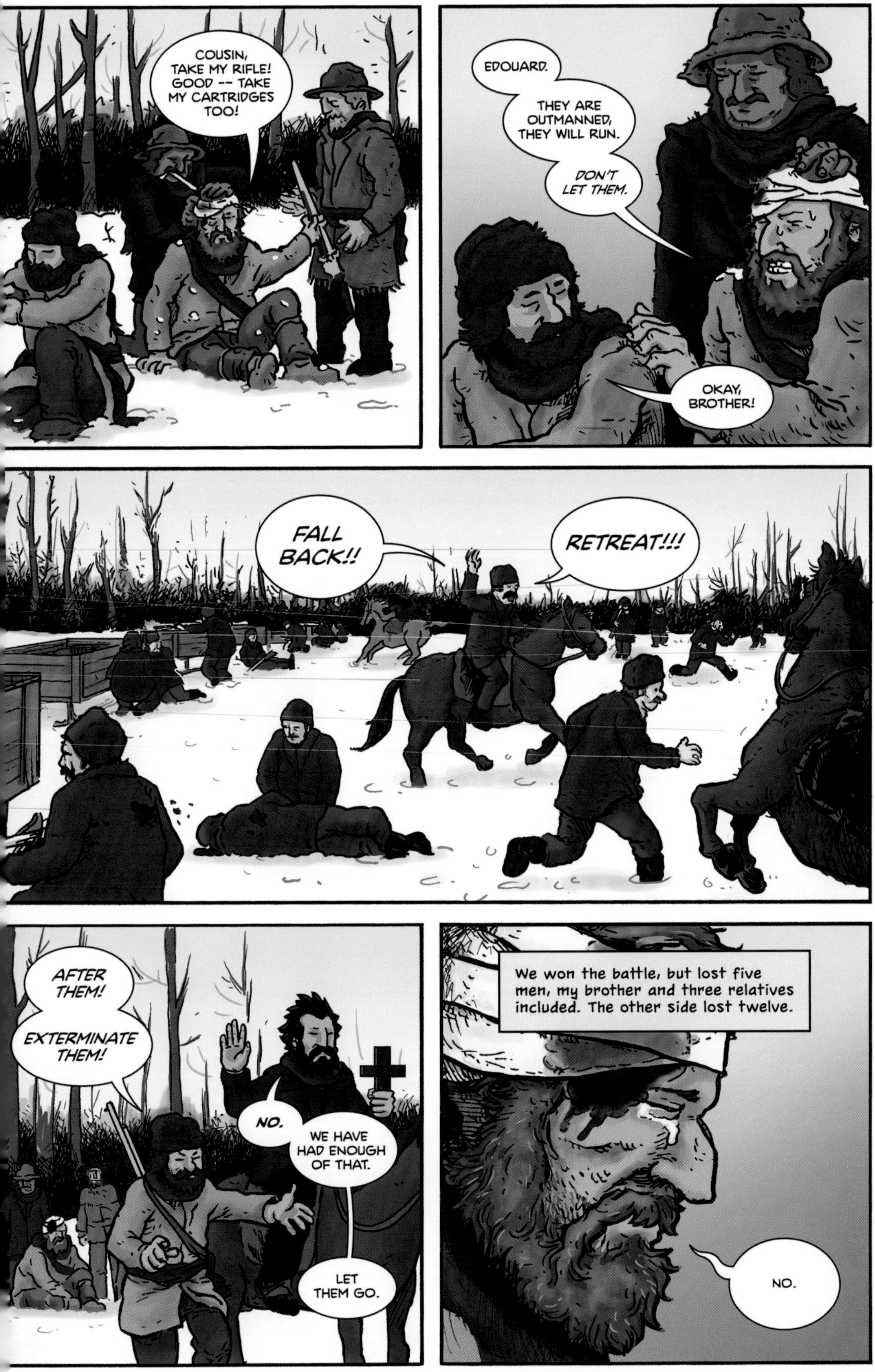
COUSIN, TAKE MY RIFLE! GOOD -- TAKE MY CARTRIDGES TOO!
EDOUARD.
THEY ARE OUTMANNED, THEY WILL RUN.
DON'T LET THEM.
OKAY, BROTHER!
FALL BACK!!
RETREAT!!!
AFTER THEM!
EXTERMINATE THEM!
NO.
WE HAVE HAD ENOUGH OF THAT.
LET THEM GO.
We won the battle, but lost five men, my brother and three relatives included. The other side lost twelve.
NO.

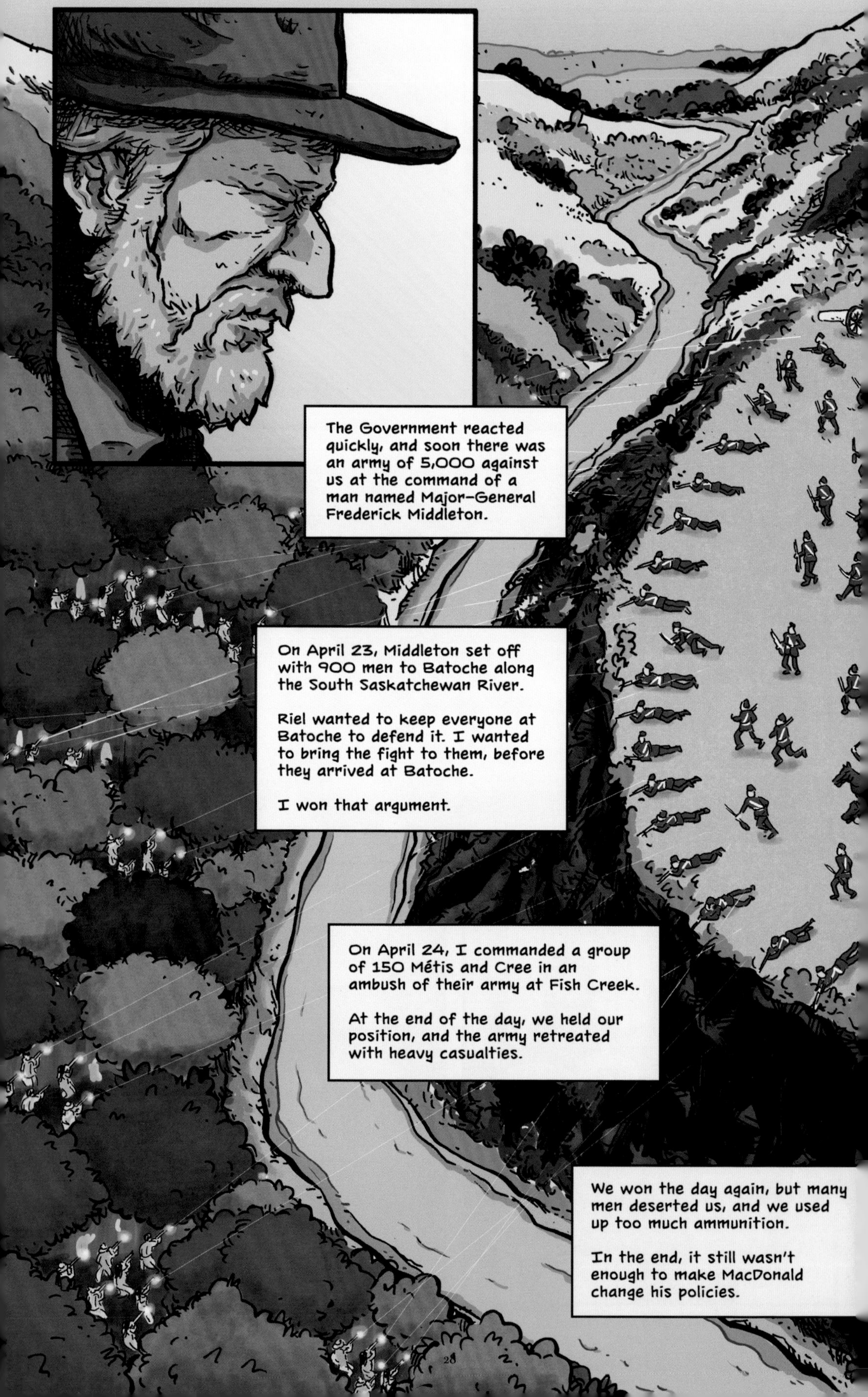

The Government reacted quickly, and soon there was an army of 5,000 against us at the command of a man named Major-General Frederick Middleton.
On April 23, Middleton set off with 900 men to Batoche along the South Saskatchewan River.
Riel wanted to keep everyone at Batoche to defend it. I wanted to bring the fight to them, before they arrived at Batoche.
I won that argument.
On April 24, I commanded a group of 150 Métis and Cree in an ambush of their army at Fish Creek.
At the end of the day, we held our position, and the army retreated with heavy casualties.
We won the day again, but many men deserted us, and we used up too much ammunition.
In the end, it still wasn't enough to make MacDonald change his policies.

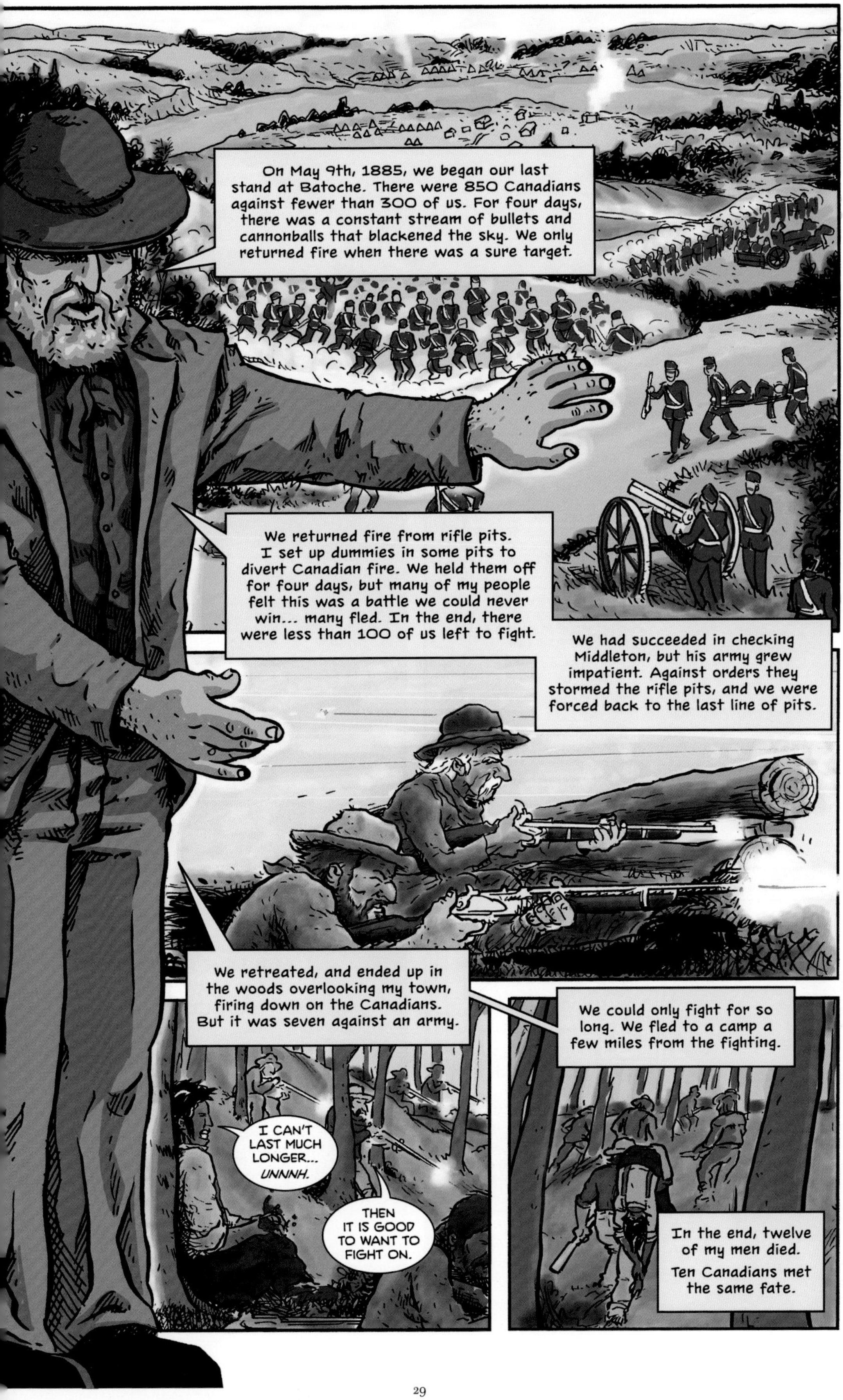
On May 9th, 1885, we began our last stand at Batoche. There were 850 Canadians against fewer than 300 of us. For four days, there was a constant stream of bullets and cannonballs that blackened the sky. We only returned fire when there was a sure target.
We returned fire from rifle pits. I set up dummies in some pits to divert Canadian fire. We held them off for four days, but many of my people felt this was a battle we could never win... many fled. In the end, there were less than 100 of us left to fight.
We had succeeded in checking Middleton, but his army grew impatient. Against orders they stormed the rifle pits, and we were forced back to the last line of pits.
We retreated, and ended up in the woods overlooking my town, firing down on the Canadians. But it was seven against an army.
I CAN'T LAST MUCH LONGER... *UNNNH.*
THEN IT IS GOOD TO WANT TO FIGHT ON.
We could only fight for so long. We fled to a camp a few miles from the fighting.
In the end, twelve of my men died.
Ten Canadians met the same fate.

I snuck around for days, harassing the Canadians when I could and looking for Riel.

Eventually I ended up at my Father's house. I told him I wished to stay the Summer around Batoche and continue to fight them from the shadows, on my own.

I AM PROUD YOU HAVEN'T GIVEN UP, BUT YOU WOULD BE A FOOL TO STAY HERE AND KEEP FIGHTING. THERE ARE SO MANY OF THEM, AND SO FEW OF US.

FATHER...

AND MAKE YOUR WIFE A WIDOW? THERE HAS BEEN ENOUGH BLOODSHED. LISTEN TO YOUR WIFE. HEAD FOR THE BORDER.

I WANT TO FOLLOW YOUR ADVICE, FATHER. I WILL LEAVE IF I CANNOT FIND RIEL.

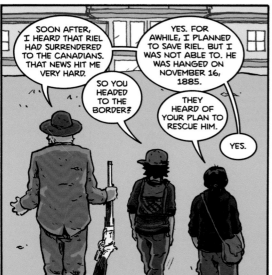

SOON AFTER, I HEARD THAT RIEL HAD SURRENDERED TO THE CANADIANS. THAT NEWS HIT ME VERY HARD.

SO YOU HEADED TO THE BORDER?

YES. FOR AWHILE, I PLANNED TO SAVE RIEL. BUT I WAS NOT ABLE TO. HE WAS HANGED ON NOVEMBER 16, 1885.

THEY HEARD OF YOUR PLAN TO RESCUE HIM.

YES.

JUST BEFORE I ARRIVED HERE, I WAS TALKING TO BILL CODY IN JUNE 1886.

I HAD AGREED TO JOIN HIS SHOW, 'BUFFALO BILL'S WILD WEST SHOW' AS A TRICK SHOOTER.

THEY WERE GOING TO CALL ME THE HERO OF THE HALFBREED REBELLION.

ALL I REALLY WANT, THOUGH, IS TO GO BACK HOME TO BATOCHE.

HE FOUND OUT HE WAS GIVEN AMNESTY ON JULY 22, 1886. THAT MEANT HE'D BE ABLE TO GO HOME.

MR. DUMONT, I THINK IT IS TIME TO GET YOU BACK TO MR. CODY.

AU REVOIR, MONSIEUR DUMONT! MERCI BEAUCOUP!

AU REVOIR, MES AMIS.